Another Pinch of Salt

by

Terry Smith

BY THE SAME AUTHOR:

'Sunshine, Sugi and Salt'

Available on Amazon Kindle

ACKNOWLEDGEMENTS

As always, to my wife, Diana, who suffered countless periods of solitude while I tapped away at the keyboard, but who was always willing to listen and make constructive suggestions when I read through a passage I wasn't sure of.

To my beloved late parents for allowing me to go to sea as a sixteen-year old, and thus gain the necessary insight to make this work and its predecessor viable.

To Rose and Bob Miles for reading the manuscript, pointing out errors and for their valued opinions regarding content.

To various publications and websites that allowed me to check dates, destinations or whatever, thus making the chronological and geographic aspects of the work as accurate as possible.

To my computer-wizard friend Paul Mallett whose contribution in preparing the work for publication was invaluable.

To Keith Mallett for his superb cover design.

And last but not least, to all those who purchased, 'Sunshine, Sugi and Salt', for the complimentary reviews and the laudatory personal messages, all of which provided encouragement for this second volume. Many thanks, indeed.

ABOUT THE AUTHOR

Terry Smith (his real name) was born and raised in the Bedfordshire market town of Biggleswade. His first love has always been railways but thanks to some superb childhood holidays on the Hampshire coast he developed an early interest in shipping - especially merchant shipping. It should come as no surprise, then, that in addition to becoming a signal-box telegraph lad (his first occupation upon leaving school at Easter, 1959) and later a railway signalman, he also served as a merchant seaman.

After a period of schooling at the training ship, *Vindicatrix* he went on to serve with the Port Line and the Blue Star Line, both of them front-line British shipping companies that sadly no longer exist. His travels took him to Australia and New Zealand and various ports *en route* - including a circumnavigation - to several countries on the east coast of South America; to Poland via the Kiel Canal when the nation was a hard-line communist state; to numerous British and Continental ports and to the Atlantic islands before they were developed as holiday destinations.

Now retired, other occupations have included factory hand, brewery operative, agricultural worker and for thirty years until Christmas 2013, mobile gent's hairdresser. He and his wife Diana now enjoy an active but relaxing retirement in a new home at Falmouth in Cornwall.

TABLE OF CONTENTS

INTRODUCTION

'Another Pinch of Salt' follows the continuing exploits of Steve Chapman, the central character of the author's previous novel, 'Sunshine, Sugi and Salt'. Therefore, as another work of fiction all persons mentioned are imaginary; so any reference to any individual (with the exception of the likes of Mimi Grey, sister in charge of the sick-bay at the training ship *Vindicatrix,* along with Mary and Charlie who really did run a gift shop in Buenos Aires) living or otherwise, is purely coincidental. The same also applies to the Confederated Argentine Steamship Company - also referred to as the Simpson Line - which is also an invention as are the vessels it operated. That said, if it had existed it would doubtless have employed its fair share of youngsters like Steve.

***

The life of a galley boy in the British Merchant Navy could at once be both uninspiring and rewarding. At the lower end of the thread he could be found peeling potatoes and preparing other vegetables; strapping up a seemingly endless assortment of kitchen equipment while simultaneously being responsible for the cleanliness and tidiness of the galley. At the other extreme he would be exploring the world, have one foot on the ladder of promotion and on attaining his rating could embark on a culinary vocation. There might follow further promotions, and if he was really ambitious then by the time he was thirty he might have reached the pinnacle of his profession. But there were also other options. He might decide to branch out into bakery, confectionery - or perhaps both. However, whichever direction he adopted it invariably depended on him passing countless exams and attaining an exemplary standard. But whatever, the horizons were boundless; and the possibility was that even the chef aboard a celebrated Cunarder could trace his roots to those humble beginnings as a galley boy.

Warning! Please be aware that for purposes of realism, passages of dialogue in 'Another Pinch of Salt' contain swearing and items that some may consider 'Non-PC'. I appreciate that such language doesn't suit everyone so if anyone is offended I apologise.

Also, some of the terms are unique to the seaman; so for the benefit of those with no seafaring experience I recommend reading the end-of-book glossary before you embark on your voyage.

PREFACE

No one could say that Steve Chapman in any way lacked ambition. For the past three months his sole *raison d'être* had been a speedy return to New Zealand and the South Island town of Manoao, to a general store and to a girl who lived there with her family.

His initial efforts had been stymied. He'd been hoping for a berth on an inter-island ferry that was being completed in a Clyde-side shipyard. On applying in person at the Union Steamship Company's office at Tower Hill in London he'd been told by a strait-laced secretary with a face like horse who'd been given half a bag of oats instead of a full one, that, "We only accept applications in writing". And then, after he'd written and posted his letter he'd received a reply stating that the company had been so inundated that no further applications were being considered. Still, he was nothing if not persistent and in the wake of this exploratory disappointment had headed for the New Zealand High Commission.

Here he was presented with another setback, for although he had aspirations of a place on the New Zealand government's assisted passage scheme, he'd learnt that without a recognized occupation he wouldn't qualify and that if he wanted to further his ambition of emigrating to New Zealand then he'd have to foot the bill for his own passage - and that could be mightily expensive.

The fares he'd been quoted were eye watering, the cheapest being offered by the Sitmar Line who for the dubious privilege of him sharing a four-berth cabin with three complete strangers, were willing to transport him from Southampton to Auckland for the princely sum of £206 single. For someone who was earning £15/7/6d a month as a basic wage and who had twenty-five quid in the bank it seemed the impossible dream, but he'd promised Maxine he'd be back and he wasn't giving in without a fight. Okay, it might take longer than he thought and a darned sight longer than he'd hoped, but he'd make that money somehow, and the position of galley boy on the good ship *Sombrero* seemed as reasonable a starting point as any.

1

It was October 1962 and Steve Chapman, a graduate of the training ship *Vindicatrix,* was two months shy of his eighteenth birthday. The event in itself wouldn't be earth-shattering; the key to the door was still three years away, when he attained the age of twenty-one - but that wasn't of immediate concern. For the present his sights were keenly focussed; on December 15th to be precise, when if all went according to plan he'd achieve his rating and with it an increase in pay. A pretty substantial increase as it happened, from the miserly pickings of a boy-rating to that of an adult crew-member, a fabulous thirty-six pounds. Okay, nine pounds a week didn't sound much, but when overtime and leave pay were factored in, and bearing in mind that he wouldn't have to pay for his keep, his financial circumstances would be easily the equal and most probably superior to those of his land-based contemporaries.

It was with that positive outlook that he strode along the road behind the sheds in the Royal Albert Dock, *en route* from the offices of the Confederated Argentine Steamship Company - also known as the Simpson line - in the Royal Victoria Dock, to the location of his latest posting. 'She's down at number three in the Basin,' the catering superintendent had said, after informing Steve that his new position would be as galley boy, aboard the company's sole remaining passenger-cargo liner. 'It's a good mile and a half so if I were you I'd take the bus.

'But Steve had opted for the walk. That way he could take in the sights whereas on the bus he'd be past them in a flash. He'd already passed the banana elevators near the Connaught swing-bridge, where *Jamaica Producer* was disgorging her Caribbean harvest.

Now here he was, beneath the elevated conveyor that was currently shifting carcasses of lamb from New Zealand Shipping Company's *Paparoa* directly from the ship to the cold stores. A hundred yards further on and there was British India's *Waroonga,* loading cargo for Cochin and Madras while at the opposite quay, Shaw-Savill's *Doric* was being manoeuvred alongside by a pair of fussing tugs on completion of her voyage from Australia.

However, not everything of note was afloat. Trainloads of goods were being shunted to and fro by the port authority's own locomotives, while laden fleets of lorries arrived at or departed from the transit sheds. A proportion of the merchandise was exports, from Chiver's jam and Cross & Blackwell salad cream to Persil, Steradent and coat hangers; in fact, anything that could be wheeled on a sack barrow. Meanwhile, heavier items, maybe motor vehicles or machine tools, were delivered directly to the quaysides and from the quaysides directly to the holds.

But exports were only part of the story and a relatively small part at that. Virtually everyone knew that Britain imported considerably more than she shipped to her overseas customers. It was also a noticeable fact that almost without exception, the vessels now occupying the sixty-odd berths in the Royal group of docks had arrived more heavily laden than they would be when they subsequently sailed. This imbalance in trade would be partially offset by what the government euphemistically referred to as 'invisibles': insurance, financial services and somewhat ironically, shipping. This latter came about owing largely to the size of Britain's merchant fleet, whereby vessels flying the Red Ensign transported consignments for any number of overseas clients, without necessarily, 'coming home'. But that was the nature of commerce and it dramatically emphasised the importance of a large and versatile merchant fleet. Whatever, 'invisibles' or otherwise, it apparently appeared that the monthly trade figures regularly registered a stubborn and unhealthy deficit.

But Steve wasn't bothered about trade figures. Politics and accountancy were for others, whereas the only financial pursuit that he was concerned with was how long it would take him to fund that ticket to New Zealand. And so he walked on, past Ben Line's *Benloyal* and *Benvannoch* and out of the Royal Albert Dock. He crossed Woolwich Manor Way, into the confinement of the Albert Dock Basin - and there lay the Simpson Line's *Sombrero*.

A two-funnelled steamship built in 1932 there had originally been three in her class although two been lost in the war. The *Fedora* and *Mantilla* now lay rusting at the bottom of the Atlantic, somewhere between the River Plate estuary and the south-western approaches to the Channel, leaving the *Sombrero* as the sole survivor. In this capacity she was vying for custom with several well-established contenders. This couldn't be a straightforward undertaking, not even for a state-of-the-art carrier let alone one of advancing seniority. The *Sombrero* was growing long in the tooth, and it was generally supposed that the company kept her going as a matter of sentiment rather than dispose of her and concentrate their resources on their half-dozen straightforward cargo liners. But keep her going they did and they did so with considerable pride. This was reflected in her paintwork - an attractive grey hull and white upper-works, the ensemble topped off with a blue letter 'S' on each of her yellow, raked funnels.

Although it was beginning to make inroads, the advent of the jet-propelled airliner had so far had only a minor impact on the passenger traffic that was traditionally transported by sea. Notwithstanding the loss of the *Magdalena* on her maiden voyage in 1949, Royal Mail had still seen fit to replace their 'Highland' class ships in the late 1950s; and although essentially cargo-passenger liners, Houlder Brothers had foreseen sufficient call to include

3

accommodation for twelve fare-paying guests aboard a couple of good-looking new-builds. Meanwhile, Blue Star were continuing to fill the seventy-odd berths aboard all of their established passenger ships with no obvious fall-off in patronage.

And so it was with the Simpson Line. The *Sombrero* was a one-class vessel with accommodation for two-hundred 'bloods', in single and two-berth staterooms. She'd enjoyed several refits; and although lacking modern air-conditioning, the provision of punkah-louvres throughout in place of the previous electric fans made her as comfortable as any of the competition.

Steve stood on the quay and contemplated his latest assignment. For twelve-thousand tons she seemed huge, her lengthy superstructure and two tall funnels giving her a more massive appearance than other ships of similar dimensions. Astern of her lay the Ropner tramp *Swainby*, while at the opposite quay sat a Norwegian freighter wearing the unmistakable colours of Fred Olsen. These humble surroundings allowed the ageing *Sombrero* to assume the role of a matriarch, something that would have been quite impossible had she lain among more illustrious neighbours.

These were the only three ships in the 'Basin' which was otherwise littered with lighters, with the greater number of them gathered towards the lock, effectively blocking the river entrance. That wasn't of concern in itself. Since the opening of the King George V Dock and its associated lock the latter had become the Royal group's principle river entrance owing to its larger dimensions, the original Gallion's entrance at the eastern end of the Albert Dock Basin being retained for emergencies or for when maintenance was needed on the former. There had once been a river entrance at the western end of the Royal Victoria Dock but this had long since been sealed, owing to its obsolete proportions.

To the north of the Basin, through gate number twelve sat the grand-looking Gallion's Hotel. A previously luxurious edifice, it had been built in the late nineteenth-century by the P&O company to accommodate passengers intending to sail on its liners. However, the years had rolled on and with P&O now embarking most of its 'fares' at either Tilbury or Southampton the Gallions had seen better days. Like many of the watering holes surrounding the docks appearances could be deceptive, and what looked so stately from without was considerably less so within. It was mostly to do with capacity. With the place often packed with dockers and seamen it was no use the landlord cluttering the interior at the expense of cash-paying clients; so furniture had been reduced to a minimum, leaving bar-rooms of barn-like expanse. Still, this was currently all academic; there was work to be done and the *Sombrero* was awaiting Steve's presence.

Hauling his suitcase behind him he scaled the precipitous accommodation ladder, the covered gangway bearing the legend 'Simpson Line' on each of its canvas flanks - and along which the passengers would eventually embark - having yet to be craned into place. On reaching the summit he found the seaman on gangway duty studiously dragging on a Player, ogling a long-legged blonde while leaning on a teak-varnished rail. The girl, a junior from head office wearing a skirt that was too tight and too short, was also struggling up the ladder clutching a briefcase full of papers for the Captain.

'You'll probably find him in the bureau,' droned the watchman, offhandedly, tossing his head in the direction of a doorway when Steve asked the Second Steward's whereabouts. And without taking his eyes from the girl, he added, 'If he ain't in there try the Purser's office.'

'In that case, where can I find the bureau?' enquired Steve, more than a little annoyed at the lack of interest shown by the person who apart from playing a security role should also have offered some guidance.

'Through that door and up the companionway,' replied the seaman, grumpily, nodding at the entrance behind him before escorting the blonde every inch of the way to the Captain. 'It's between the shop and the hairdresser's - if you don't get lost along the way.'

Bollocks to you, thought Steve, ignoring the sarcasm and stepping into the superstructure where he was confronted with carpeted opulence, I'll remember that bastard if I ever get to serve him his dinner.

It was clear at a glance that the *Sombrero's* owners weren't niggards; at least, not towards their fare-paying entourage. Sumptuous armchairs surrounded the foyer while expensive-looking artwork embellished the timber-work panelling. To both port and starboard alleyways extended for virtually the length of the superstructure, each of them home to comfortable and outward-facing staterooms. From the centre of the concourse a carpeted companionway ascended to the next deck above. Steve was surprised at the stairway's shallowness, a feature almost certainly for the benefit of the passengers who would be totally unaccustomed to the more usual steeply-inclined ladders. Whatever, the area was deserted as Steve, taking a renewed grasp of his suitcase, headed in the direction of the companionway.

Upon reaching the top he discovered yet another piazza with further longitudinal alleyways. It was off these alleyways that the remainder of the staterooms were situated. They were also home to the dining saloon; the Purser's accommodation and office; the various public rooms and their associated bars; and the ancillary spaces - the aforementioned bureau, hairdresser's and shop, along with a well-equipped surgery.

Again, the entire area seemed deserted. Steve paused to admire a painting of the *Mantilla* that had been commissioned to celebrate her launching. On the opposite bulkhead hung a similar portrait of the *Fedora,* whilst the canvases were surrounded by pictures of the *Sombrero* herself, in her present guise and as a wartime transport. Everything oozed luxuriance; and it was a well-known fact that the food served to Simpson Line passengers was singularly fare *par excellence.* However, it remained to be seen just how generously they treated their crews.

'Looking for someone, Son?' asked a voice from apparently nowhere as Steve, startled by the intrusion, glanced fore and aft and to both port and starboard in search of the elusive utterance. And then he caught sight of a movement; a reflection in the glass of the framed depiction of the *Fedora.* He took a few paces forward, past the hairdressing salon and there was the bureau, a timber-panelled, brightly-lit office with a lengthy and highly-polished counter. Behind the counter stood a slight, bespectacled figure with a balding head and with a cigarette dangling from his lips.

'Hello! I'm looking for the Second Steward', said Steve, as the fellow regarded him from over his spectacles which were perched on the end of his nose. 'Wouldn't be you by any chance, would it?'

'It might be,' replied the other, lifting a flap at the end of the counter and stepping out on to the carpet. It all depends why you're asking.'

'I'm the new galley boy,' answered Steve, who now spotted the zigzag on each of the leading hand's epaulettes, 'and I've been told to report to you by the office.'

'Okay - but there's not much doing at the moment,' replied the other, withdrawing the ciggy from his mouth and wiping away a strand of tobacco. 'As you can see, there's hardly anyone aboard. Apart from a handful of stewards who are tidying up the passenger accommodation and a few deckies aft there's only a cook and a scullion. The rest of the crew'll be turning up sometime tomorrow. Oh! I nearly forgot. There's the Old Man and the Chief Engineer - but they usually eat in their cabins. Anyway, that's not your problem. Follow me and I'll show you to your room and then you can get changed into work gear.'

Steve played 'follow my leader', down the staircase and another companionway until they arrived at the ship's working alleyway. This corridor, noticeably more spartan than the others, extended aft along the starboard side with cabins to the left and a lengthy row of lockers to the right. Roughly mid-way along it veered inboard, by a couple of feet, suggesting that the cabins beyond were larger than those further forward. It was to these apparently more spacious rooms that the Second Steward appeared to be heading, until they reached the third from the end where he stopped and flung open the door. 'This is your billet,' he articulated, ushering Steve through the doorway. 'Chuck your gear on one of the bunks while I go and sort you out some linen.'

The cabin's external appearance gave the impression of a spacious interior but it was clearly an optical illusion. Rather than the two-berth affairs that Steve had been used to this one accommodated four, so although it was dimensionally larger in terms of personal space it was cramped. The timber-framed bunks were of two-tier construction and were set in a single block of four. They stood against the forward bulkhead, one pair adjacent to the porthole the other two nearer to the door. A quartet of lockers stood opposite; whilst a leather settee filled the remainder of the bulkhead and the space beneath the wide-open porthole. Drawer space was beneath the two lower bunks, one apiece for each of the four occupants, whilst a coffee table completed the furnishings. As for ventilation; apart from the porthole it was dependent on a pair of punkah-louvres either side of the central light-fitting, with smaller examples at the head of each bunk in close proximity to the reading lamps.

Steve had been spoilt something rotten - and it wasn't just the good old *Alice Springs*. Port Line were equally to blame. Over the summer he'd completed a couple of voyages with the company; a 'run' from London to the Tyne and a trip to Gdynia in Poland. Both vessels, the *Port Townsville* and the *Port Melbourne,* had been beautifully appointed, with single-berth rooms for all senior crew with two-berth cabins for the boys. He could see at a glance that the *Sombrero* was a different proposition, and he wondered how he'd cope in this less indulgent, more confined environment. But then, he thought, it wouldn't be for long and if it didn't work out he could always move on to something new; there were plenty of other companies to choose from.

'Hey! Are you coming to collect this bed-linen, or do you want me to make up your bunk?' Steve started - it was the Second Steward calling from the linen locker, and the scoffing pronouncement caused a warning light to flash in his head. What was it with this ship, he thought, as he hurried out into the alleyway. I've only met two of the *Sombrero's* crew and they've each been guilty of 'sniping'.

The Second Steward was standing at the linen locker with an armful of sheets and pillow-cases. In addition to the linen there were a couple of towels and a large bar of carbolic soap. 'Take this lot and make up your bunk,' he ordered, 'and then, when you've changed into working gear and stowed away your kit you can report back to me at the bureau.' That appeared to be that; he'd already secured the locker and seemed about to depart when he hesitated and quietly enquired, 'This your first time on a passenger liner?'

'Y-y-yeah,' stuttered Steve, as he was about to head back to his cabin beneath the burden of bed-linen, 'but I'm not sure it's what I expected.'

The Second Steward smiled, shaking his head in wonderment. 'That's one thing you'll have to get used to. Generally speaking it isn't so cushy aboard these ships. For a start, there's a lot more bullshit than on the cargo boats. But one thing in your favour - you'll be cooking for the deck and engine room boys so you'll have very little contact with the posher sorts. Have you ever worked in a galley?'

'No,' replied Steve, who was beginning to wonder if the Second Steward's bite might not be so scathing as his bark. 'I've only worked in pantries up till yet, but I'm guessing there's not a lot of difference.'

'Well, I can tell you straightaway that there is,' answered the Ducer, as second stewards were colloquially referred to aboard passenger ships. 'For one thing there'll only be the two of you - yourself and the Ship's Cook - so you'll only have each other for company. But for now you'll be working in the main galley, alongside Derek and Jim. Then tomorrow, when the rest of the crew report, you and the Ship's Cook'll be shifting aft and stay there until you hear otherwise.'

'Where is the Ship's Cook?' asked Steve, who'd previously only heard reference to the two who were already working.

'Ashore on the piss, I shouldn't wonder,' came an answer that was laced with contempt. 'He turned up this morning, dumped his bag in his cabin and we haven't set eyes on him since. He'll get a fuckin' rocket when he does show.' Steve digested this item with stoicism, wondering just what kind of mate he'd been saddled with.

Hmmm, thought Steve, eyeing the lower bunk nearest the porthole which was already made up with a magazine lying on the counterpane, that must be Jim's so I'd better grab one of the others. In the event he chose the upper berth closest to the door, reasoning

10

that with the porthole open and the door on the hook it would benefit from better ventilation.

Having made up his bunk he changed into dungarees and T-shirt, hanging his shore-going clothes in the nearest of the three vacant lockers. It was then simply a matter of unpacking the remainder and stowing it in one of the drawers. He checked his pockets for cigarettes and lighter. Everything was there; so with his now empty suitcase standing upright in his locker he headed on back to the bureau.

'Right, I'll take you down to the main galley and introduce you to the lads,' offered Sec, shuffling a sheaf of papers and laying them flat on the counter. 'Fuckin' passenger list, he grumbled, nodding despairingly at the pile of neatly-typed documents. Drives you fuckin' nuts trying to work out where to accommodate them - especially when there are eight fuckin' kids.'

'Kids?' queried Steve - he hadn't even considered that children might form part of the passenger manifest - but then he realized it was inevitable if families were among those on passage.

'Yeah, kids,' answered Sec, as he led the way downwards and then through a network of alleyways. 'They're a fuckin' sight worse than bloody animals - and they're like a plague of locusts at mealtimes. And the parents, especially the more toffee-nosed ones, haven't a clue about controlling their brats. In fact, one of the owners and his tribe are actually sailing with us this trip. Going to Montevideo to buy some show-jumping horses by all accounts. There'll be four of them altogether - the mother, the father and their offspring. The eldest one's a right little bastard. Still, I suppose when he's old enough they'll pack him off to Eton and he'll end up as fuckin' Prime Minister. Right! Here we are - this is where you'll be working till tomorrow.'

They'd arrived in a brightly-lit rectangle that glistened with highly-polished steel. The fluorescent-tube lighting accentuated the brilliance which made for a light and airy setting. This was the *Sombrero's* main galley, and very impressive it looked too with a host of labour-saving gadgets. Steve immediately recognized the 'rumbler', a potato-peeling device that saved an awful lot of labour. There was an electric chip maker and a food mixer, the only thing missing - it appeared - being some kind of electric washing-up apparatus; a fact exemplified by a tall, gangling fellow with a shock of blonde hair who was up to his elbows in soapsuds.

'Hey! Jim!' called the Second Steward, gesticulating with a beckoning index finger. At the sound of his name the scullion - a derogatory term for a Cook's Assistant - strolled easily towards them, flicking hair from his eyes while drying his hands on a pantry cloth. 'This is........what's your name?' asked the Second Steward, turning to Steve, having suddenly realized that there'd been no sort of formal introduction.

'Steve - Steve Chapman,' answered Steve, nodding at Jim who responded with a big, cheesy grin.

'Steve - Jim, Jim - Steve,' continued the Second Steward, as if the lapse had only been temporary. 'He's never worked in a galley before so perhaps you can show him the ropes. He'll be moving aft tomorrow, to the crew galley - that's assuming that useless bastard of a Ship's Cook doesn't go adrift in the meantime.'

'Sure, Sec - no worries,' answered Jim, 'I'll make sure he gets the hang of it. And as for the Ship's Cook - I saw him heading for the 'Gallions', but I dunno where he might have gone since.'

'That's all we need,' replied the Second Steward, rolling his eyes as if seeking divine intervention, 'another bleeding piss-artist. I was hoping this bloke'd be different. We had enough trouble last trip. I had to sort out a couple of punch-ups after the cook got plastered and the dinner got burnt to a frazzle - and the galley boy was just as fuckin' bad. Glaswegians, they were, and they just couldn't stay off the grog.'

12

The clatter of tinware drew Steve's attention to the bakery where Derek, the Second Cook, was busy making rolls, bread and pastries. 'We haven't got a baker at present,' offered Jim, nodding in the direction of the bakery from where profanities were issuing as the baking tins were noisily recovered, 'so Derek's been lumbered - the cooking, the baking........the lot. I'm helping out where I can but I can't do everything. But I can see the Ship's Cook getting a bollocking - whenever or if he turns up.'

'Still, you'll be all right tomorrow,' replied, the Second Steward, as if the shortage of manpower was just a minor hiccup rather than a fully-blown headache. 'The rest of the lads'll be reporting for duty and that'll bring you back up to strength.'

That's if everything ran smoothly. Today was Monday and the remainder of the hands should all be aboard by lunchtime tomorrow at the latest. They were due to sign articles on the Wednesday with the *Sombrero* sailing on the Thursday. It didn't allow a great deal of leeway; but with many of the crew - especially the catering staff - being 'regulars' it shouldn't cause too many problems. However, that was assuming the more wayward fraternity, of which the Ship's Cook was a classic example, didn't bugger things up in the meantime.

Steve was quickly aware of a difference in the crew's composition, especially in the catering department. For a start there'd be no chief cook. In charge of the galley was a qualified Chef who was answerable only to the Purser. There was a second cook, third cook and assistant cook, a couple of scullions; while an additional galley boy took care of the strapping-up and cleaning. There were chief and assistant bakers; and a butcher, whose shop was adjacent to the bakery.

Topside, a Purser ruled the roost - and everyone involved with the catering. There were barmen; deck, bedroom and smoke-room stewards; 'wingers' - and three assistant stewards who catered for the uniformed hierarchy. There were also a pair of stewardesses whose primary functions were the care and well-being of the lady passengers, especially those travelling solo. There were a total of five pantry boys; three topside, under the supervision of a pantryman with the other two manning the officers 'and engineers' pantry which was adjacent to their dining room and accessed via a hatch from the galley. Quaintly, but perhaps owing to the *Sombrero's* age, the topside pantry was serviced by a rope-propelled elevator.

With regard to the stewards; those presently aboard were mostly either Portuguese or Spanish. They were engaged on a contract basis, serving for four consecutive trips before taking an entire voyage off. Those with leave owing would disembark at Santander or Lisbon to be replaced by a corresponding number of their countrymen. They'd rejoin the ship at the end of their leave, when the *Sombrero* next called at those ports.

The surgery was the domain of a superannuated, hospital consultant who - according to him - was a survivor of the *Titanic* disaster. Whatever, given his nervous disposition it was the perfect excuse to guzzle bucketful's of gin, supposedly for medicinal purposes. Thankfully, his subordinate, the Sick-Bay Assistant, was a fully-qualified nurse who was totally abstinent and the mainstay of the surgery's function. To complete the line-up there was a nanny, a gorgeous brunette who was only engaged when babies and toddlers were sailing. Her little realm, the gaily-decorated nursery, was at the forward end of the lower promenade deck, thankfully well out of earshot.

Apart from the Captain, Senior Radio Officer and Purser, the nanny and the stewardesses were the only crew to be accommodated in the passenger area, not only to be close to their charges but presumably to segregate them from the males; although it was widely rumoured that in the course of the previous trip one of the stewardesses had been given a 'jolly-good seeing to' by the Sparky.

'Tell you what,' said Jim, as Sec disappeared leaving Steve to be tutored by the scullion, 'you get stuck into that strapping up while I get this veg in the steamer, otherwise there'll be sod all for lunch.'

Steve had taken to Jim instantaneously. The fellow had a cool temperament, precisely what was needed in tight situations such as lunch being left in the balance. Steve was also pretty sure that this wealth of composure combined with an amicable nature would make for a flourishing friendship. In fact, once Derek had got the bakery under control and its produce in the oven the preparation of lunch was a cakewalk. Okay, so it wasn't the five-course blow-out the *Sombrero* was renowned for but there was plenty, and an escalope of veal with veg and potatoes followed by rhubarb and custard was sufficient to keep everyone happy.

'Fancy a pint?' asked Jim, eventually, sliding his empty plate across the coffee table and slumping across the settee (they'd decided to eat in their cabin, it being a lot less austere than the mess-room). 'There's still half an hour till closing time, and we can finish the cleaning down afterwards.' And so that's what they did, slipping ashore and through gate number twelve to the near-empty Gallions Hotel.

'That's him,' murmured Jim, beneath his breath, while nodding at a fellow at the end of the bar who was chatting with a middle-aged female. 'Looks like he's had a skinful already.'

'That's his ninth,' whispered the barman, as he pulled two pints of bitter then held out his hand for the cash, 'and her ladyship there is sinking them a bloody sight faster.'

Her 'ladyship', whose make-up appeared to have been applied with a trowel, was from the prefab settlement of Cyprus, a tiny community at the rear of the Royal Albert Dock. Like the errant

Ships Cook she was obviously bladdered and totally oblivious of her surroundings.

'We'll be lucky to see him again,' said the scullion, as he sipped from his pint of Ben Truman (they were sitting at a beer-stained table some way from the bar from they could study proceedings discreetly). 'He'll be fit for sod all in the morning.'

'Thought I'd find you in here,' said another voice as Derek, who'd mysteriously appeared from nowhere, drew up a chair and plonked his pint down on the table. 'Anything to report on matey, there?'

'No - only that he's as pissed as a newt,' advised Jim, as he reached for his matches and fired up an Export Woodbine. 'In fact - as I was saying to Steve, the way he's going on I don't think we'll be seeing him tomorrow.'

As if to confirm the prophecy there was an almighty crash from the end of the bar and the Ship's Cook, along with his female acquaintance, collapsed on the floor, saturated with ale and giggling like a pair of silly children. 'Right, that's enough for you two,' voiced the barman, stepping from behind the bar and hauling the woman vertical before propelling her doorwards where she promptly tripped over the doorstep. 'And you can join her,' he added, ignoring the prostrate form and turning to the Ship's Cook who'd risen shakily and was aiming a swing at the speaker. The would-be hay-maker missed by a mile but had the inevitable consequence of throwing the assailant off balance. He ended up on the floor and was dragged to the door where he lay floundering on the ground near his girlfriend. But following several attempts they managed to haul themselves upright - a wobbling and reeling sort of upright - and after hurling obscenities at the barman, staggered mazily off towards Cyprus.

And as for the barman; he wore a self-satisfied smile as he dusted his hands in the wake of a job well accomplished. His only concern now was that Steve and his companions should finish their pints so

16

that he in turn could get some shut-eye. This was owing to the early-morning dockside licensing hours, meaning that apart from a couple of hours between eight and ten the pub had been open since dawn. 'Time gentlemen, please,' he bellowed, yanking on a lanyard at the rear of the bar causing a bell to give resonance to the call. 'We're open again at five-thirty so you don't have to wait till tomorrow.'

'Come on, let's drink up and get out of here,' said Jim, grinding out the butt of his Woodbine in one of the battered Old Holborn tins that served as ashtrays in the Gallions, 'We'll not get any peace until we do.'

And so, what of Steve's work as a galley boy? Well, it was early days and he'd had merely a taste of what the job might have to offer. As the Second Steward had so aptly conveyed, it was so completely removed from pantry work which had included an element of stewarding. He was going to be busy, obviously, with meals being prepared to a strict timetable. A one o'clock dinner, for instance, meant exactly that unless it was altered for a purpose; a conflicting sailing time, for example, although that only happened very rarely. On a more positive note, there wasn't the bullshit that reigned routinely in a pantry. Okay, the galley staff had to be presentable; but if for instance an item of apparel became soiled in the course of his duties he wouldn't have to change it immediately. It would do at the end of the day whereas in the pantry, whatever the time or circumstance, all clothing had to be spotless.

That evening, Steve, along with Derek and Jim, took a taxi to Plaistow and the celebrated 'Green Gate' tavern, a pub that was noted for its talent contests. Although Derek was content just to sit with his pint Steve and Jim were more enterprising, taking to the stage with a passable rendition of Jimmy Dean's, 'Big, Bad, John'. It was received with generous applause, so given the ovation they initially believed their performance had won them the money. However, victory was claimed by a pint-sized comic with his impression of 'cheeky', Max Miller. The lads couldn't complain as the finale was an absolute blast, and included the gag that had seen the inimitable Max banished by the BBC.

The following morning there were shocks, for when Steve turned to it seemed Jim's clairvoyance had been flawed. It wasn't yet 6.00 am, but rather surprisingly the erratic Ship's Cook was already at work and heating up a large pan of porridge. 'Hello, Sonny Boy,' came the cheerful greeting as Steve stood gazing in amazement. 'I'm Michael........Michael O'Connor, and I guess you're either a scullion or a galley boy.'

'Um - er - galley boy, actually,' answered Steve, quickly recovering his composure. 'And if I'm not very much mistaken I'll be working with you in the crew galley.'

'Well, I don't see that being a problem - do you?' answered the Irishman (for an Irishman he was without a shadow of a doubt as Steve had discovered in the Gallions) with a big-hearted grin that suggested he was far more likeable than the guy who'd taken a swipe at the barman. 'I'm sure we'll make a wonderful twosome.'

Steve wasn't fully convinced; but he'd take things as they came for at the end of the day, almost everyone deserved a second chance. Derek and Jim were caught equally off-guard; but given that Michael was working like a slave they too seemed ready to forgive - regardless of the fact that 'Paddy' had let them down only yesterday.

In fact, Michael's good humour was so infectious that within a very few minutes all four of them were laughing and joking, the previous day's misdeeds forgotten. As the morning rolled on the remainder of the galley staff reported until by eleven o'clock the place resembled Piccadilly Circus. It may have been a pretty large galley but a dozen incumbents, all milling around and in each other's way, made it uncomfortably overcrowded; and so, with the crew galley due to be mobilized Michael asked the Chef for the key. The Chef, a tall, slim Portuguese who gloried in the name of Frederico Henrique Silvares, handed over the requisite article - but made no mention of what it concealed.

As previously related, the main galley was a well-equipped show-piece, the only impediment from Steve's point of view being the aforementioned dearth of a dishwasher. However, the crew galley transpired to be different, more in keeping with the *Sombrero's* archaism. An outpost at the stern of the ship, abaft the petty officers' quarters and above the deckhands' and engine room crew's accommodation, it was a throw-back to the age of the tea-clipper. Steve couldn't believe it as he surveyed what was essentially a Victorian kitchen, complete with a coal-fired cooking-range. The associated coal bunker - set into the after bulkhead - had recently been replenished, but by either design or accident the hatch at its foot was agape. And that posed their very first problem; the coal had spilled out and every surface was coated in coal-dust.

More positively, unlike the main galley which was located amidships and relied on artificial light, the crew galley was blessed by Mother Nature. You see, to both port and starboard there were stable-type doors that opened on to a teak-timbered deck. So, whatever the shortcomings they were adequately compensated for by fresh air and daylight and the freedom to roam as they pleased.

'The bastard responsible for this ought to be condemned to life in a Siberian coal mine,' opined Michael, as he studied the mess they'd been left with. 'Well, one thing's for sure,' he declared, rolling up his sleeves and taking hold of a bucket and coal shovel, 'we'll not be cooking anything today. You'd better nip back and tell Frederico-Henrique what's happened - and that the main galley'll have to feed us all.'

19

In normal circumstances, owing to the absence of an elevator, the peggy would bring an armful of dixies to the top of an internal companionway, collect the food and then place it in the mess-room hot-press - only today that procedure had been eclipsed. Instead, the embattled peggy would have to traipse half the length of the *Sombrero* with the aforementioned dixies before carrying the food back to the mess-room. By this time it would probably be cold, would take a good twenty minutes to reheat and so become a recipe for a riot.

'Tell you what,' called Michael, as Steve set off on his errand, 'if you hang about a minute I'll write out a list of the stores we'll be needing - and if you wipe the coal-dust from some of those baking trays', he added, nodding at a collection of kitchen accoutrements that were stacked in a corner, 'you can use them to carry the stuff on.'

Steve was wondering just how the Second Steward would react, having to reopen the stores for Michael's benefit in addition to the early-morning opening time; and bearing in mind the character's bristly nature, he voiced his concerns to his workmate.

'Don't you worry about him,' replied Michael, apparently not caring a monkey's. 'If he kicks up a fuss just tell him to come and see me.'

Huh! thought Steve, as he descended the starboard companionway to the after well-deck and made his way forward through the working alleyway, it's all very well Michael dishing out his instructions, but he won't be in the firing line if Sec's in a shitty kind of mood.

But he needn't have worried for as he ambled along he noticed that the dry-stores were open; and there was the Second Steward, issuing sugar and tea to the pantryman while others stood waiting in line. Steve joined the queue and when it came to his turn he presented his list of requirements.

'Fuckin' hell!' exclaimed the leading hand, studying the portfolio which was almost as long as his arm. 'You got a wheelbarrow for this lot?'

'Well, we are starting from scratch,' replied Steve, not at all impressed by the outburst, 'and the lockers and fridge are all bare.'

'Well - they would be, wouldn't they?' answered the Second Steward, brusquely, as he reached for a large bag of rice, 'seeing that they're emptied at the end of each trip.'

Ignoring the sarcasm Steve was quick to change the subject. 'And another thing,' he declared, gaining in confidence by the second, 'the place is knee-deep in coal dust.'

'Must have been that galley boy last trip,' came the answer, when Steve related how the coal bunker's hatch had been left open. 'What a useless fucker he was. I've only known you for twenty-four hours but I'm hoping you'll be an improvement.'

Well, I suppose that was some sort of compliment, thought Steve, as he made his way round to see Frederico-Henrique with his trays piled high, one balanced shakily on the other. He knew he'd have to make a return journey, to collect the meat, fish and butter from the butcher, not to mention a pint or so of milk; but first he had his message to deliver. As expected, it went down like a concrete balloon but it couldn't be helped and the Chef could either like it or lump it.

But thinking seriously it could have caused problems owing to the differing meal times; dinner and tea, for example, as opposed to luncheon and dinner. It was sometimes argued that the varying definitions were a form of discrimination, identifying the officers and passengers as being socially superior to the crew. Whatever, the men didn't seem overly bothered, eating breakfast at eight, dinner at one and tea at five-thirty precisely. It will be noticed that there is no reference whatsoever to luncheon. This was a meal served exclusively to the uniforms and fare-payers and was generally taken at twelve-thirty. This would be followed by a four o'clock afternoon tea with dinner at seven on the dot. Anyway, as everyone knew, luncheon wasn't eaten by working people. To them, lunch was a mid-morning snack, to sustain them through the lengthy period between breakfast and the midday meal. And as for additional sustenance; there was always plenty of bread and butter, cheese and jam, etc.; in the mess-room if the men became peckish between times.

Message delivered and foodstuffs collected Steve waded into the cleaning, assisting Michael in restoring their galley to something of an acceptable order. Okay, it could never be likened to that aboard ships like the *Canberra*, nor a great many others for that matter; but by the time they'd finished - with the hatch at the foot of the coal bunker firmly secured and only open when it was needed - they could feel pretty satisfied with their efforts.

In the event, thanks to their exertions, the men did get their teas as per schedule and a cracking good tea it was too. There was ham and pea soup for starters with fresh, crusty rolls from the bakery. This was followed by beef curry and rice with fruit salad and ice cream for afters. There were no complaints so omens for the future seemed promising.

'Well, I'll be leaving you to clean down, then,' announced Michael, sliding his empty dinner plate into the sink when he and Steve had finished eating. 'I'm off to Cyprus to spend the evening and overnight with Vera.'

'That the - um - er........lady I saw you with in the Gallions yesterday lunchtime?' enquired Steve, not quite sure how he should phrase the question.

'That's her,' answered Michael, with an all too obvious gleam in his eye. 'She may be showing her age but she's an absolute humdinger. I've known her for yonks - and she doesn't charge me for her favours.'

As Michael hurried off to get changed Steve took stock of their eating arrangements which were primitive solely by choice. No separate messing facilities were provided for the Ship's Cook and galley boy, it being assumed that they'd eat with the crew. However, after weighing their options they'd decided to eat in the galley, balancing their plates on their laps while seated on upturned saucepans. 'Leaves us open to abuse - eating with that lot,' Michael had explained as he swallowed a mouthful of curry. 'Taking the piss out of the cook is one of the deck department's favourite pastimes.'

Steve was warming to Michael, and despite the Irishman's obvious liking for liquor he was sure that they'd get along fine. The man was plainly no fool and wouldn't be a butt for stuff and nonsense. He was also clearly an excellent cook, so there shouldn't be any cause for insults.

On the Wednesday morning, in the period between ten o'clock and noon, articles were signed in the officers' and engineers' dining room. And then, during the early afternoon, and with the *Sombrero* being a passenger ship, she - or rather her crew - was subject to a Board of Trade inspection. This pre-voyage review involved both fire and boat drills with the outboard lifeboats being lowered. Initially it was a trouble-free exercise. The fire drill was performed without mishap; but when it came to lowering and rowing the lifeboats in order to convince the inspectors that the *Sombrero's* crew were able and competent boat handlers, it declined into an absolute shambles.

In order to accommodate her entire complement with capacity to spare the *Sombrero* carried half-a-dozen lifeboats. Steve was in lifeboat number four, the middle of the boats on the port side and one of the three to be lowered. The Second Mate - a highly-strung fellow at the best of times - was in charge, and by the end of the drill he was on the verge of a nervous breakdown. All went well until the keel touched the water and the craft was released from its falls. It was largely the result of indiscipline that sent the officer almost, if not entirely, off his rocker.

Steve had been rowing before - mostly in dinghies around the lake in the park near his home; while some of the others - the deckhands especially - must have shown some sort of boat-handling expertise in order to have obtained their certificates. Lack of coordination was the problem, with few pulling as one, some catching crabs; while several of the stewards held the oars as if they were pairs of dirty knickers. The boat spun around on the spot. The poor Second Mate was going blue in the face while those observing from the *Sombrero* - the inspectors excepted - derided and jeered which contributed to the growing sense of chaos. Eventually, after a second launching during which proceedings ran a little more smoothly, the inspectors seemed satisfied and the shenanigans were brought to a close.

'Well! I'm glad that little fiasco's over,' offered Michael, as he and Steve returned to their galley to begin preparations for tea. 'Robbed us of some afternoon shut-eye, that has - and for what? It'll be just the same next trip - and the trip after that. The trouble is the crews are never together long enough to form any kind of cohesion. Still, there's sod all we can do about it,' he added, as he stirred a pot that had been gently simmering since breakfast, 'so let's make this steak and kidney pie.'

In order to cook effectively on the antiquated range a clean and hot fire was essential. The onus for this was on Steve and it included the care and maintenance of the appliance. He'd stoked up the fire and closed down the dampers before leaving the galley for the drills. Now, with the dampers reopened he ruttled the coals and they instantly flared into life.

He'd spent part of the morning peeling spuds, a quantity of which he loaded into a pot that Michael placed on the stove. As you've probably guessed, there was no electric rumbler in the crew galley. Instead, first thing every morning after collecting the stores he'd start peeling the necessary potatoes. With no seat to sit on he squatted on an upturned pot, peeling the potatoes and tossing them into a water-filled milk churn. The churn in turn served as a storage vessel until whenever the potatoes were needed. In effect he'd be peeling sufficient potatoes for both dinner and tea (a hundredweight, no less, every day) for the entire eight weeks of the voyage. Down in the main galley, after the rumbler had performed its ten-minute miracle, the couple of milk churns that were utilized for storage bided their time in the handling room, a division of the domestic fridge complex. Up here in the crew galley there was no equivalent storage space so the potatoes were cooked on the very same day they were peeled. Any left over were used for the following day's breakfast, perhaps for bubble and squeak or the ever popular corned-beef hash.

And so, steak and kidney pie, freshly-cut greens and potatoes; not a bad stomach lining for those embarking on a final night's carousing before heading for the South Atlantic.

Most of the crew were already ashore and Steve was in the process of changing. Suddenly, a clanging of bells and shouts of alarm persuaded him to look out of the porthole. The clamour of bells heralded the arrival of an ambulance and a madly-driven Wolseley police car. They were making for the Dutch freighter *Jonker* that had taken up the berth that had previously been occupied by the *Swainby.* Steve hurried aft, still buttoning his shirt, for a more detailed view of the action. Staring from the taffrail he saw a man being fished from the water by the crew of a tug who were using a boat-hook as a grappler. Once safely on the tug he was transferred ashore and into the waiting arms of the ambulance men. The ambulance then sped off, its bell jangling, while the police ascertained a sequence of events from the tug crew. It later emerged that the fellow, a crewman from the *Jonker* and a notorious dipso, had been weaving his way along the quay, had tripped over a bollard and swallow-dived into the basin. Luckily for him the tugboat crew, having heard the splash and seen him thrashing about had speedily raced to his rescue. Owing to their presence of mind he was now on his way to the Albert Dock Seamen's Hospital to undergo the pleasures of a stomach pump.

So, with the excitement over Steve set off back to his cabin. He was halfway down the companionway to the after well-deck, still fiddling with an awkward shirt button, when something pulled him up in his tracks. Call it what you will: extrasensory perception, a sixth sense, feyness or whatever, a voice was telling him that while he was up here he ought to check up on the galley. Fortunately he had the key in his pocket so he unlocked the doors on the starboard side and switched on the fluorescent light. The galley was locked overnight as a deterrent to casual pilferers, but there was no sign of a break-in or trespass. He could see at a glance that the fire was still smouldering and that everything was shipshape and orderly, so what could have caused his foreboding. Hmmm........must be me getting windy, he thought, as satisfied that all was as it should be he switched off the light and was about to slam the door shut behind him. And then a glint caught his eye in the gloom. He reopened the doors and switched on the light and there sat a black-and-white cat. So, that's what he'd spotted - the cat's eyes shining in the dark. 'Goodness me! Where on earth have you come from?' he asked, stooping to stroke the feline which rubbed around his legs in an obvious display of affection. 'Well! You can't stay in here,' continued Steve, picking up the animal and cradling it in his arms where it purred like a finely-tuned engine. 'I'll take you ashore in a minute and then you can find your way home.' And then he glanced down at his shirt. The garment - or at least the front of it - was as black as the night and in no fit state to be worn. So, that's how the cat had got in, through the hatch on the top of the coal bunker. Whatever, his shirt was a mess and the cat faced immediate eviction.

'Saw it happen myself, once - well, the aftermath at any rate,' announced Derek, as he wiped the head of his beer from his moustache. He, Jim and Steve were sitting in The Roundhouse, discussing what could have been 'curtains' for the Dutchman. 'We were up in Hartlepool at the time, aboard an old tramp called the *Maywood*. Cor! talk about fuckin' rough - but that's another story. Anyway, me and my mate were returning to the ship when we spotted this little gang of onlookers. They were staring at some bubbles in the dock. Well, before you could say Jack Robinson up pops this smelly, black body. And talk about fart - it was all full of gas, just like a bleedin' politician.'

'Yeah.......well, go on - tell us the rest of it,' prompted Steve, who was desperate to hear the story as it happened, minus Derek's silly witticisms.

'Well, it seems he was a Somali fireman off one of the colliers', explained Derek, ignoring Steve as he warmed to the crux of his tale. 'Not that we'd have been able to tell cos they reckon all these bodies - even albinos - are as black as the Ace of Spades when they've spent any time in the water. Anyway, he's apparently been ashore on the piss, fallen in the dock and drowned without anyone knowing. As it happened there were no witnesses and it was assumed at the time that he'd simply gone adrift and would turn up again sooner or later.......and that's what he did, come to think of it.'

2

Thursday dawned pleasantly warm; the sun was shining so all things considered they couldn't have wished for anything finer. The covered gangway along which the passengers would embark had already been positioned; while the blackboard at the head of the accommodation ladder proclaimed that the *Sombrero* would be sailing at two o'clock precisely with shore leave expiring at noon. But passengers were of no great concern; well, not to Michael and Steve who'd carry on as normal, catering only for the needs of the crew. Down in the mess-room the men helped themselves to cereals, toast and marmalade while porridge and a full English breakfast was prepared in the galley and duly collected by the peggy. The seven-bell breakfasts had already been dispatched and Steve was busy scraping carrots.

He'd turned to at six; had reopened the dampers so that the fire was well ablaze; had collected the stores and had already peeled half a sack of spuds. He'd peel the remainder during the morning; between his other chores, such as cleaning the galley and strapping up the odd pot or pan. Perhaps tomorrow, or maybe on Saturday, he'd polish the stove so that it shone brightly for Captain's inspection which was scheduled for eleven o'clock, Sunday.

But first things first. With the crew safely fed and the carrots in a pot he laid out some bacon in a tray. Another tray, this one containing half-a-dozen sausages, was already sizzling away on the lower shelf of the salamander while Michael was at the stove frying eggs.

'Can't beat a good breakfast,' announced the Irishman, cheerfully, flipping a couple of the eggs leaving the other two 'sunny-side' up.

'Sets you up for the rest of the day so that you can enjoy your lunch-time with a pint.'

Steve chuckled. He too appreciated a good breakfast and readily acknowledged that since becoming a seaman - not counting the weeks he'd spent at the Vindi where the food had been appalling and sparse - the full English version had become commonplace. Whether it was doing him any good or not was a different matter. He was aware of an increase in his weight and his clothes were fitting tighter than they should. He knew he'd have to do something about it eventually; all things in moderation - isn't that what his parents had tried to drum into him? But 'eventually' didn't mean today. Nevertheless, at home, although there was always plenty of food on the table, a fried breakfast was a Sunday morning treat.

They were now into their third day in this outdated galley and there was a question that Steve needed answering. 'Any idea why we've got a coal-fired stove while virtually everything else on the ship is electric?' he enquired, as he dunked a slice of fried bread into the juice of his plum-peeled tomatoes.

'Well, I'm no electrician,' answered Michael, between alternate mouthfuls of fried egg and sausage, 'but I believe it's to do with the current. It's the same aboard older ships in general. As far as I'm aware there's nothing to convert the current from DC to AC, and I'm thinking there may be insufficient voltage up here at the stern to power an electric cooker. If that's the case then the only solution that I can see is to install a sub-station in order to boost up the current. As it stands, though, and given the Sombrero's age, I'm guessing the company regards it as more economical to continue buying coal than invest in a current converter.'

'I can see your point about her age but I'm not sure I'm any the wiser,' replied Steve, who didn't know the difference between an amp and an ohm but to whom electricity was conveniently available by simply flicking on a switch, 'but I guess you know what you're talking about.'

'As I said' replied Michael, wiping a smear of grease from his chin. 'I'm no electrician, but I think that's got to be the answer.'

As it happened the passengers were late arriving, three of them having got lost while making their way to the pick-up point at the Simpson Line's passenger office in Regent Street. They eventually arrived in a quartet of coaches but happily with an hour to spare. Steve was wondering if it was really worth the company maintaining a West-End passenger office when apart from the *Sombrero* they only possessed a couple of passenger-carrying freighters. He concluded that it must be a matter of prestige as it didn't make any sense otherwise.

The *Sombrero* sailed as per schedule. As previously related, rather than use the lock in the eastern wall of the basin she exited the Royal Group via the lock at the seaward end of the King George V Dock. Her tugs drew her forward, through the swing-bridge spanning Woolwich Manor Way and into the Royal Albert Dock. From here she was manoeuvred stern first, through the cut linking the Royal Albert Dock with the King George V Dock and thenceforth into the river. In less than an hour she was heading for the sea and the excitement of Samba and Tango.

Steve had posted a mailing list to his parents the previous evening: well, he'd posted three mailing lists actually as he'd also mailed one to Maxine in New Zealand and another to his maternal grandmother. The lists had contained the agents' names and addresses at the various ports in the *Sombrero's* itinerary. These included Santander on the north coast of Spain; Lisbon in Portugal; Teneriffe in the Canary Islands; Recifé, Rio and Santos in Brazil; Montevideo in Uruguay and finally Buenos Aires, the capital city and principal port of Argentina. What an exciting prospect, he'd thought, as he read through the list of destinations. Dark-eyed señoritas, goodness how many sorts of exotic refreshment along with weeks of sunny weather.

By late afternoon the *Sombrero* was butting her way down Channel with the weather rapidly deteriorating. There was a gale blowing and according to reports from amidships the majority of the passengers had taken to their cabins and looked likely to dispense with their dinners. There were no such problems for the crew and tea was despatched with typical seafaring gusto.

With the *Sombrero* at sea Steve spent the evening with his room-mates. In addition to Jim there was Colin, the other cook's assistant, and the midships galley boy, a fellow from Sunderland called Alan. Alan had an acoustic guitar, and the pre-bedtime hours were spent warbling out songs with Alan strumming a lively accompaniment. It was improvisation; but impromptu sing-alongs were a popular way of passing the off-duty hours, especially among the younger generation. Meanwhile, others sought their own amusement - like the next-door neighbours, for instance.

The next cabin aft was home to a foursome of stewards who flaunted their homosexual lifestyle. On one occasion, when Steve had been passing and their door was ajar, he'd taken a peek and had been greeted with, 'Come on in, Ducky - we don't bite. Fancy a lager and lime?' That had been George, one of the bar stewards who preferred to be known as Georgina. Georgina and his companions were a splendid crowd, as generous as the day was long; and weren't over-pushy so long as you stressed that you didn't indulge in their form of social activity.

And what about the Hairdresser, a dapper little mortal called Gerald who shared a two-berth cabin with the Shopkeeper - a mismatch if ever there was one? You see, Gerald was queer but the Shopkeeper wasn't so Gerald was out on a limb. In view of this he spent most of his leisure time with Georgina to whose circle he was a welcome addition.

Then there were those who lived quietly and were more than content with perhaps reading, yarning or making up a foursome at cribbage. In fact, Steve was something of a bookworm, enjoying Westerns mostly, by the likes of Louis Lamour and Max Brand. The novels were usually well thumbed and had changed hands on countless occasions as part of a shipboard exchange system.

And what can we say about the Laundryman, a chain-smoking, anti-social Scouse who seldom went ashore but spent his theoretical off-duty hours laundering crew-members' shirts? He charged twenty fags a shirt so was clearly on a nice little earner.

A character who seemed something of a loner was the Writer, a position of indeterminate distinction but loosely attached to the catering department. He was what some might describe as the 'Ships Secretary', responsible for keeping records and accounts as well as carrying out most of the typing duties. Whatever, he kept largely to himself in his cabin-come-office at the after end of the officers' and engineers' alleyway.

The gale persisted for much of the crossing of the Bay of Biscay while the rainfall was an absolute soaker. But on the third day out the elements relented and on the morning of their arrival at Santander the sun shone brightly while the sea state was greatly improved. Far to the south-west Steve could see what he thought was a huge bank of cloud, towering upwards like the aftermath of a massive explosion. But the closer they came to the Iberian coast the clouds transformed into the mountains of the Pecos de Europa, so christened by early Spanish explorers as it was the first land they sighted on returning from their overseas exploits.

It was just about noon when they entered the harbour at Santander, past the magnificent Magdalena Palace which had once provided a summer retreat for the Spanish Royal Family but now served as a faculty of learning.

Michael was slaking his thirst with the Donkeyman while Steve kept an eye on the dinner. He was more than content with this arrangement, so long as there weren't any hitches. You see, although he'd only been in the job for a week he was learning the rudiments of cooking; notwithstanding that it was on a coal-fired range rather than a posh electric cooker. For instance, he knew when the potatoes were boiled by simply pricking them with a fork; and the same went for most of the other vegetables although he wasn't quite so sure about greens. Whatever, all seemed well until something in a corner caught his eye. He just gawped in amazement for there, watching from the shadow of the coal bunker, was that confounded black-and-white cat.

'I don't believe it!' he exclaimed, as the animal stared back, its only reaction to Steve's obvious surprise being - well, no reaction whatsoever. 'I definitely put you ashore on Wednesday evening so how on earth did you find your way back?'

'Probably up the gangway when the watchman was fast asleep,' offered Michael, who was standing at the top of the mess-room companionway cuddling a can of Tuborg. 'He's a bit of a useless bugger, that one.'

'But what do we do now?' asked Steve, stroking his chin while trying to think of a solution. 'We can't just dump him ashore,' he continued, assuming the creature was a male, 'and hope someone here looks after him.'

'Then it looks like he'll have to stay with us,' answered the cook, who admitted to having a fondness for cats, especially black-and-whites whose personalities were apparently unique.

'But what if there are any complaints - from the Purser, for instance?' persisted Steve, who wasn't entirely convinced that adopting the cat was a brilliant idea even if it sounded attractive.

'He's a miserable bugger at the best of times so he's bound to raise an objection.'

'There won't be any complaints - you wait and see,' replied the cook, over his shoulder as he ambled to the rail and tossed his empty lager can overboard, 'least of all from the Purser.'

Steve could see that it was no use arguing and became resigned to the fact that henceforth there would be three in the galley - at least during the hours it was open; and perhaps the cat could earn his keep as a rat-catcher, although he had to confess that as far as he knew the *Sombrero* was 'rat-free' territory. 'What are we going to call him, then?' he asked, as he rubbed the cat's head and ran his hand along the animal's back before sliding its tail through his fingers. 'If we're going to keep him he's got to have a name.'

'Whisky! That's what we'll call him,' answered Michael, re-entering the galley and lifting the lid of a saucepan that was on the verge of boiling over.

'Whisky? What kind of a name for a cat is that?' demanded Steve, who clearly imagined that Michael had responded with the first word that had entered his head. 'I can understand a ginger cat being called Marmalade, or a black cat being called Sooty - but Whisky? Where's the connection between a black-and-white cat and - Whisky?'

'Well, isn't it obvious,' replied Michael, who was gleefully enjoying Steve's discomfit. 'Black and White? Whisky? Get it?'

Steve looked perplexed; but eventually, after racking his brains and scratching his head, the penny dropped and his features lit up with a grin. 'Yeah, you're right,' he answered, stroking the cat with a fondness that was clearly appreciated if the purring was anything to go by. 'From now on we'll call him Whisky - and judging from the racket he's making I'm guessing he's agreeable too.'

The *Sombrero* tied up in the very heart of Santander's commercial district, just across the street from an assortment of bars, bodegas and offices. Ahead of them lay the Pacific Steam Navigation Company's *Cotopaxi,* while astern sat a rusty Spanish tramp, of indeterminate origin but possibly of Victorian vintage. The name on her counter professed her to be the *Don Pedro Ramirez Garcia.*

The immediate port area occupied a long stretch of wharf that backed directly on to the business quarter which itself appeared relatively modern, the result it transpired of a disastrous fire that in the nineteen-forties had destroyed many of its earlier components. Nevertheless, considerable thought had gone into the replacement architecture causing the ancient to blend with the new. It meant that with a backdrop of hills - and the fact that the city was strung out along the shores of a bay - the vista was quaintly picturesque.

After dinner, having cleaned down the galley and banked up the fire, Steve took a walk in the sun; not to patronize any of the bars or bodegas - he hadn't any Pesetas and didn't know where to change his money - but for a stroll along the Avenida Rein Victoria. This was a broad and attractive boulevard that hugged the coast beside a succession of beaches before coming to an abrupt end at a cluster of rocks in the district of Sardinero, close to the city's casino.

At this stage of her history, Spain, although still in the grip of the 'Franco Dictatorship', was slowly emerging from the dark days of hunger and poverty that had blighted the nation for decades, a transition that would eventually see her evolve as one of Europe's most prosperous and influential democracies.

But today, despite the sunshine and warmth there was a paradoxical greyness that defied any clear-cut explanation. The people appeared sad and subdued; maybe as a result of the ongoing suppression that still denied freedom of speech. But whatever, at least there was Sardinero, with its snow-white casino, elegant dwellings, colourful gardens and gloriously sun-kissed beaches. For years a popular destination, this splendid locality would rapidly become one of the finest of Spanish resorts.

Back at the *Sombrero* Michael had been busy with the Tuborg as the stack of empty lager cans testified. That said he wasn't incapable and tea was coming along nicely - even if a shade premature. For whatever reason he'd misread his watch and the meal it appeared would be ready much sooner than scheduled. Fortunately, the menu was largely sympathetic. There was Scotch-broth for starters with a main course of sweet and sour pork. It wouldn't hurt the soup to simmer longer - nor the pork either for that matter; it was the rice that was the spanner in the works. It was already boiling in the pan, and in maybe ten minutes would be ready to serve before it descended into mush.

When Steve brought the error to his notice Michael reacted instinctively. He made a grab for the pan, to remove it from the heat in the hope that the rice wouldn't spoil. But, in his haste - not to mention his tipsiness - the water slopped over, scalding his hands and causing him to howl like a baby. Whisky shot out of the galley, his face reappearing almost immediately as he peered around the door to determine the cause of the uproar. Meanwhile, as Michael plunged his hands into a bucket of cold water Steve moved the rice from the heat, to the edge of the stove before closing the dampers as a precaution. 'Better get you to the Surgeon,' he proposed, as Michael, his agony partially assuaged by the water, gradually came to his senses.

'I guess you're right,' he agreed, as the damage to his hands became manifest, 'I can't carry on like this. Looks as if from now on you'll be doing most of the cooking - for the time being at any rate. They'll not be able to spare anyone from the main galley - but you'll be okay if I supervise.'

Steve wasn't totally persuaded; but first things first - he had to get Michael to the surgery. It was remarkable how quickly he'd sobered, and Steve stated as much as he led the Ship's Cook, blistered hands dangling, out of the galley and down across the after well-deck.

'Yeah? Well - you keep quiet about this,' whispered Michael, as they made their way up through the passenger accommodation which thankfully was almost deserted. 'If the Purser finds out I'll be liable for a fine and a logging.'

Steve had no intention of spilling the beans and was hopeful his mate had learnt a lesson. Still that was forgotten as they arrived at the surgery and reported to the Sick-bay Assistant. As it happened the Surgeon was out, sampling a gin with the Sparky; probably as well as the Sick-bay Assistant was a more sober and more able practitioner. And thanks to his expertise they emerged from the surgery within minutes, Michael with his hands in bandage and Steve in a bit of a tizz.

'I told you,' persisted Michael, as he wiped his nose on the back of his bandaged right hand, 'it'll be all right. You're leaning to cook faster than I ever thought likely - and with me to guide you through the trickier bits what on earth could possibly go wrong.'

'So long as you stay off the piss,' added Steve, sceptically, but who if the truth was known was looking forward to this unofficial posting, additional workload excepted. 'And you'll have to muck in where you can.'

In common with most in her itinerary, Santander was one of those ports where the *Sombrero* called only briefly. A small amount of cargo was handled and a few extra passengers embarked; but the principal reason for the visit was mail. Like most British liner companies the Simpson Line had a contract with the Post Office, ensuring a regular and speedy transfer of post in the days before airmail dominated. So, come eight o'clock, once a handful of Spanish stewards had been replaced by a clutch of fellow nationals, the *Sombrero* sailed, heading for Portugal and Lisbon.

3

As the *Sombrero* headed west towards Cape Finisterre, Whisky settled down in his 'bed'. The contrivance, an old cardboard box with the sides reduced and with an empty sack for a mattress it was an example of Irish ingenuity - prior to Michael's mishap. Inevitably, it wasn't long before the moggy's existence was an open secret. But if anything his presence was welcomed; and given that the Captain was a lover of cats not even the Purser had the nerve to dissent. Rather, Whisky rapidly became a celebrity and a much-loved 'member of the crew'. He thrived on leftovers and handouts and never wandered far from his adopters. He slept in the galley which although admittedly warm was also conveniently well ventilated. So, with a bowl of milk and the occasional cream treat he became a very pampered pussy indeed.

As luck would have it Michael's injuries weren't major. It was the backs of his hands that had borne the brunt of the scalding while the palms were relatively unscathed. His fingers protruded from the bandages so he wasn't completely helpless but there wasn't a lot he could cope with. So, Steve was suddenly in the limelight, accomplishing whatever Michael couldn't; like chopping vegetables, concocting sauces, carving joints - in fact anything requiring nimble fingers. Okay, the cook could just about manage to feed himself and he drank his tea through a straw; but one thing he couldn't do was hold a can or a glass, a bonus if ever there was one.

Galley grapevine or galley telegraph, call it whichever you prefer; but news travels fast aboard ship as exemplified the following morning when Steve went in search of the stores.

'You getting on all right up there?' asked the Second Steward, when Steve handed him the barely legible list that Michael had scribbled with an awkwardly-held stub of pencil. 'Only I heard that the Ship's Cook was in a pretty bad way and couldn't even wipe his own arse.'

'No, we're managing okay,' replied Steve, being economically truthful without actually resorting to lies. 'He scalded the backs of his hands while moving a pan of hot water but he isn't an invalid.'

'Wasn't pissed by any chance, was he?' pressed the Second Steward, suspecting a degree of cover-up.

'Not that I'm aware of,' replied Steve, this time lying through his teeth; and mentally cursing the Sick-bay Assistant who obviously couldn't keep his mouth shut. 'Just one of those things as far as I know - could have happened to anyone.'

He left the Second Steward guessing, but made a mental note never to trust the Sick-bay Assistant. The guy might be good at his job but where patient-confidentiality was concerned he clearly showed the discretion of a foghorn.

The *Sombrero* rounded Cape Finisterre soon after the midday siren. By early afternoon she was approaching the border between Spain and Portugal; while during the evening and overnight periods she negotiated her way through a fishing fleet. 'Sardine fishermen,' observed Jim, as he and Steve leant on the taffrail enjoying a pre-bed cigarette. 'Apart from their lights they're invisible - but the boats are tiny, and they pitch and roll all over the place when the men are hauling in their nets.'

Steve had a vision of weather-worn fisher-folk, similar to those on the north Norfolk coast where crabs and lobsters were the objective rather that sardines and pilchards. 'Rather them than me,' he opined, pinching out his ciggy and tossing the dog-end overboard. 'I'd have a job staying upright.' That said, his romanticism also

40

extended to a plethora of tight-knit communities strung out along the Portuguese shore, waiting for their men to return. Viewed from that angle the fishermen's lives seemed idyllic - occupational hazards excepted.

Lisbon can rightly be described as a city of sublime elegance; clear from the start as the *Sombrero* passed classy Estoril and entered the waters of the Tagus. With the crew at their dinners Steve and Michael became tourists as they slid past the 'Torre de Belém' - or as the English would say, the 'Tower of Bethlehem' - an elaborate fortification built in the sixteenth century as a deterrent to marauding buccaneers.

A little further on they passed the magnificent Monument to the Discoveries, only recently erected and dedicated to the Portuguese navigators who'd sailed from the Tagus to discover much of the world as we know it. Steve held those seamen in awe. They'd sailed uncharted waters in small wooden ships, not knowing when, if ever, they'd return. There must also have been the fear, especially before it was firmly established that the earth wasn't flat, that they'd sail off the edge of the world.

Further on still, standing back from the river and surrounded by woodland loomed the original, 'Estádio da Luz' - or the 'Stadium of Light', as the English pronounce it - home to the Benfica football club. The setting was ideal; so what better place to watch your favourite team give a footballing lesson to their rivals?

The view from the ship was superb as the *Sombrero* continued her progress. There was so much to see that Steve wasn't sure where to look; but his mind was made up when over to starboard rose a true colossus, both in size and religious significance.

Completed as recently as 1959, the monument - known locally as 'Christ the King' - is similar to that of 'Christ the Redeemer' which overlooks Rio de Janeiro. It took years to erect and includes an observation platform from which sight-seers can appreciate the view. As expected, it is also a focal point for pilgrims, both native and those from overseas.

Lisbon - or Lisboa, to give it its Portuguese title - occupies much of the northern side of the river and is spread over numerous hillsides. The view from the *Sombrero*, now almost in the heart of the city, was stunning as the sun played on colour-washed buildings, either of pink or white, with shallow-pitched, red-tiled roofs. As for access to the southern shores of the river: no bridges spanned the Tagus in those days. Instead, a procession of ferryboats plied to and fro with the frequency of an underground railway.

As recently related, stopovers at ports *en route* to Buenos Aires were usually of short duration, seldom lasting longer than twenty-four hours and often for a good many less. No subs were granted, the men having to rely on whatever they already possessed and could convert into the local currency. Most - Steve included - had drawn an advance on their pay when signing articles so they wouldn't go short; and as nearly everyone knew, in places like Lisbon Sterling was readily accepted in exchange for Portuguese Escudos. Fortunately for the crew of the *Sombrero,* she wasn't due to sail until early next morning so an evening on the town lay in waiting.

'You going ashore?' asked Steve, as he and Michael observed the mooring operations as the *Sombrero* was nudged alongside, between the Portuguese freighter *Beira* and a Panamanian rust-bucket called, *Jennifer.* 'I can hardly wait. I've never been to Lisbon before, and according to all accounts the women are supposed to be fabulous.'

'No, I shan't be going ashore,' answered Michael, his voice betraying genuine regret. 'There's not much point, not with my hands in bandages - and anyway, I'm not much bothered. I've been here before, loads of times, and, yeah - it's okay, but it's not as good as Rio or Santos. And as for the women - it depends which women you're talking about. If you're lucky enough to find a respectable young thing then all well and good, but if you're referring to those in the bars, the percentage girls and so on, then you'd better be keeping a lookout. It's your money they're after and before you know it you'll be skint. And another thing - nearly all of them are rotten with the pox.'

As Michael sloped off for some shut-eye Steve settled down to the strap up. He was eagerly looking forward to some shore leave but had decided he wouldn't go alone. Rather, he'd wait till this evening and tag along with his cabin mates because Jim at least knew the layout. And so, the afternoon was a non-event, with Steve just content to loaf in the sun and watch others getting on with their work. In this latter respect the process of discharging and loading proceeded steadily, the dockers and stevedores aiming to complete and meet the early-morning deadline.

It was like feeding time at Regent's Park Zoo. In order that they could get ashore as speedily as possible the off-duty crew quickly gobbled their teas and were gone in the proverbial flash, none of them worrying about the poor old peggy who was left scurrying around to get finished. Steve, meanwhile, was also in a hurry, so that he too could get ashore with his mates.

He'd banked up the fire and was sweeping up the dust when a cough interrupted his work-rate. Whisky was immediately 'all ears' while Steve spun around on his heel. He found himself confronted by a middle-aged nun who stood in the port-side doorway, smiling and swinging a pail. The woman, who was slightly built, traditionally attired and with a crucifix strung around her neck, was beaming through her wire-framed spectacles. Steve just stood there immobile, wondering at the reason for her presence. The nun proffered her bucket, as if inviting Steve to come and fetch it; the trouble was, what was he expected to do with it? She obviously couldn't speak English and he didn't speak Portuguese so there followed an uncomfortable impasse. The nun displayed signs of frustration, shaking her bucket while Steve became totally confused. Eventually, he took the receptacle and began filling it from the tap - but what did she want with the water?

'She wants you to fill it with food,' came a voice from the opposite doorway, and from where the Lamp-trimmer had been watching with amusement. 'There's another one down at the main galley. They come from a local orphanage, and go from ship to ship every night of the week collecting leftover food for the kids. She'll be over the moon if you fill it with scraps from the rosie.'

Steve thanked the Lampy for acting as intermediary and began filling the bucket with what he hoped would be gratefully received.

'I wouldn't be too fussy if I were you,' continued the Lamp-trimmer, on seeing that Steve had ignored the rosie and was loading the bucket from the fridge, 'if they're hungry they'll eat anything they're given.'

That's as maybe, thought Steve, as he continued to fill the bucket, but I wouldn't want to eat anything that had been in a rubbish bin so why should the poor bloody kids.

The nun had barely gone on her way, smiling broadly and with her bucket brimming when another face appeared at the doorway, this one more swarthy and sporting a bushy moustache. The face belonged to a shabbily-dressed fellow of debatable age who was carrying a battered old suitcase. Before Steve could object he'd opened his case on the worktop, inviting Steve to view its contents.

'Pleez! You buy a souvenir of Lisbon - a gift for your wife, maybe - help feed my family?' The case was full of gilded ornaments; and the voice was so pleading that Steve, who hadn't even got a wife but who was already feeling sorry for the bloke, was tempted to reach into his pocket so that he could purchase a gilded statuette.

'Ignore him,' advised the Lamp-trimmer, who'd stayed to make a fuss of Whisky before making his way ashore with the Carpenter who was already waiting patiently at the gangway. 'He's probably got a bloody great limousine parked behind one of the warehouses, and it's mugs who buy this shite who've paid for it.'

'Sorry,' apologized Steve, heeding the Lampy's advice and standing back from the suitcase, 'No Escudos.'

Steve didn't know if he'd pronounced the name of the Portuguese currency correctly or otherwise, but the statement had been true and it had the necessary effect. The salesman, seeing that the Lamp-trimmer was equally disinterested, latched up his case and departed, muttering something or other which Steve guessed was highly unflattering.

'Tell you what,' said Jim, as they dived between the traffic and across some railway tracks as they made their way into the city, 'we'll take a look at the sights - Black Horse Square, and so on - and then think about going for a drink. We've got plenty of time so we needn't tear about like the clappers.'

'So long as we don't get lost and miss the ship,' cautioned Alan, partly in jest but also with a hint of pessimism. 'We'll be right in the shit if that happens.'

'We won't get lost,' assured Jim, as they made their way into the best-known gathering place in Lisbon. 'All you've got to remember is that if you're walking downhill then you're heading in the direction of the waterfront.'

Huh! thought Steve, keeping his mouth shut but weighing up a possible scenario. A fat lot of good that'll do us if we arrive at the quay and find that the *Sombrero's* sailed.

But after visiting Black Horse Square, admiring the statue of King Joseph and a selection of other notable landmarks, all caution was thrown to the wind as they indulged in some Portuguese delights.

They wandered through narrow, cobbled streets - dodging brightly-coloured trams that rattled and squealed, up hill and down and around impossible curves - sampling some fabulous, locally produced ice cream, before descending on a bar called, Carlo's.

'This'll do for starters,' said Jim, as he pushed through the door flourishing a One-Pound note that the barkeeper changed without question but doubtless at a healthy commission. 'We'll have a couple in here and then carry on somewhere else.'

Steve stared around as the barman served the beers that fizzed and sparkled while music played softly in the background. The lighting in Carlo's was dim; but the décor was appealing with seating in cubicles, apart from the stools that they occupied. The place wasn't full - perhaps half-a-dozen patrons, themselves included; but it was early yet, by Portuguese standards at any rate and later it'd likely be crowded. A handful of girls - hostesses, or whatever - were huddled at the end of the bar, smoking and chatting; although Steve espied one, a raven-haired beauty with dark, smoky eyes, take a fleeting glimpse over her shoulder. He averted his gaze and engaged in some banter with his mates; until he sensed a presence - and a whiff of scent that a second ago he hadn't noticed. He turned to find the brunette beside him. He smiled - a little sheepishly, but said nothing, trying his best to ignore her. But the girl moved closer and began rubbing her leg against his. Steve reddened but didn't object. Instead, he felt utterly at a loss as the girl purred, seductively, 'You buy me a drink, Johnny, then we go jig-a-jig.'

He'd been propositioned before, most openly at the Club International in Gdynia back in the summer, but this was different. In Poland, the girl, an overweight blonde with the hem of her skirt a couple of inches higher than her stocking-tops, had adopted a 'take it or leave it' attitude, and Steve had elected to leave it, whereas the brunette was more pushy and less likely to take 'no' for an answer.

'Give her the elbow - tell her you're broke,' murmured Jim, as he expanded on Michael's earlier caveat. 'She, and the rest of them, are employed to lure clients into buying them drinks at astronomical prices. Of course, you buy one for yourself at the same time - but what you don't know is that while you're drinking spirits, or whatever, she's drinking pop even though you've paid for a brandy. Before you know it your money's all gone and you're too bloody pissed to go jig-a-jig.'

Steve pushed the girl's leg away. 'Sorry, no Escudos,' he muttered, diffidently, although he'd thrilled to the warmth of her thigh. It was that phrase again - but there was no doubting its obvious effect. Steve's pronouncement, although hesitant, had the desired outcome and she drifted off back to her colleagues, doubtless feeling cheated as she mumbled a string of profanities. 'Thanks for that,' acknowledged Steve, as Jim settled back on his stool. 'Trouble is, I don't like being rude to people.'

'I bet she's heard plenty in her time,' answered Jim, sardonically, as he lifted his glass and studied the bubbles in his beer. 'obscenities, insults - the lot. Still, if she only scores once then she's laughing for the rest of the evening.'

And that, after visiting a selection of other 'cosy nooks', was Lisbon. The *Sombrero* sailed as per schedule with only one crewman adrift, an incapable fireman who'd had an argument with a tram and been whisked to the casualty department. There was no hope of finding a replacement, which meant the Second Engineer had the major headache of having to rearrange the watches. That wasn't easy given that most of the black gang were sloshed, leaving the few who were sober to cover. These in turn were miffed to say the least at being lumbered with the additional workload.

47

4

Steve had a stinking hangover, and if it hadn't been for his mates who'd shaken him awake he'd likely have slept through the morning. That said, he wasn't alone in feeling lousy. As he made his way to the galley across the after well-deck there were others in similar straits, nursing mugs of tea and sucking in great draughts of ozone. By this stage of the voyage the stormy waters of the more northerly latitudes were rapidly fading into history. Instead, rather than tempests howling through the rigging there were zephyrs of sub-tropic air, clearing the sinuses and - with the assistance of tea - helping restore one's vitality.

Michael had turned to on the dot, with a crystal-clear head and hands that appeared to be healing. If that was the case, and provided the Sick-bay assistant was in agreement, he hoped to dispense with the bandages and said as much to Steve over breakfast.

Steve could see where Michael was coming from. It wasn't so much that his hands seemed to be healing as the fact that he couldn't hold a can. 'That's as maybe,' replied the galley boy, brighter now after a couple of codeine had performed their customary magic, 'but if the sores become infected they'll be worse than they were in the first place.'

'Even so, I'll sound him out, see what he says,' answered Michael who wasn't about to be dissuaded, 'but if he thinks it better to keep the dressings on, then so be it - I'll not be doing anything stupid. I just thought that the sooner I could get back to normal...........................'

At a cruising speed of around eighteen knots it would take approximately forty-one hours to cover the eight-hundred miles or so to Teneriffe. It would give the *Sombrero* an arrival time at Santa Cruz, the island's capital and principal seaport, of around six o'clock the following evening; so, once again, an evening ashore lay in prospect.

Steve's hangover was rapidly forgotten; and as for Michael, he returned from the surgery as happy as a pig in slurry, the bandages reduced to a basic covering, a guard against possible infection.

'He reckons they've dried up nicely,' he announced, referring to the blisters that only three days previously had been both open and weeping as well as unbearably sore. 'He says that if they carry on healing at this rate then tomorrow he might discard the dressings completely and expose the wounds to the atmosphere.'

'At least that means we should be able to resume some sort of normality,' replied Steve, as he scraped busily away with his potato peeler, 'so long as you stay off the booze. I don't mind learning - in fact I'm all for it. But you've got to remember that I'm only the galley boy, not the chief cook, bottle-washer and dog's body. And another thing - I'm only on fifteen quid or so a month, not fifty-odd or more like you are.'

Michael chuckled. 'Don't you worry, Sonny Boy, he answered, now rolling himself a cigarette with little if any inconvenience, 'I'll see you right come the end of the trip - and you'll have learnt how to cook.' Steve grunted, showing scant gratitude; notwithstanding that rolling Michael's cigarettes was another job he could erase from his 'to do' list.

The following morning an awning was rigged around the poop - not only for the benefit of the petty officers but also for those in the galley. The work was carried out at the instigation of the Mate who knew that in the heat of the tropics the awning's protection would be vital. In its exposed position - and given its all-steel construction - the after deck-house would rapidly assimilate with a sweat-box. In fact, Steve had already taken to performing many of his tasks in the open air and as a result had acquired a good suntan. However, with the advent of the awning he could perpetuate the practice without being frazzled to a cinder.

It was another of those mornings that seemed to be the rule off the coast of Spanish Sahara. The sky was blue, the sea was calm and a southerly breeze - some of it created by the *Sombrero's* headway - prompted Steve to manoeuvre a full churn of potatoes close to the starboard rail where it was exposed to the slightly cooler air-stream. Trays containing bacon, black-pudding and sausages were sizzling beneath the salamander while Michael was busy frying eggs, whistling merrily - when Steve spotted something at his feet.

The 'something' turned out to be a fish of sorts that Whisky had discovered on his travels. As it happened the cat had retrieved it from the after well-deck, decided it worthy of 'trophy' status and had set it down close to the galley. Steve bent over to examine the specimen and was amazed by its freakish appearance.

'It's a flying fish,' observed Michael, who'd witnessed the episode and was smiling at Whisky who seemed ready to pounce should either he or Steve attempt to snatch it. 'It probably leapt aboard during the night, became stranded and that's how Whisky came to find it. One thing's for sure, he certainly didn't catch it.'

Steve grabbed the creature before the cat could react, almost allowing it to slither through his fingers before he finally had it in his grasp. He took hold of its pectoral fins and opened them, displaying it to its full extent so that its shape became virtually cruciform. The 'wingspan' was quite remarkable, easily the equivalent of its body length. It also had an unusually long tail that Michael suggested might act as a rudder when airborne. He also added that the fish had almost certainly been attracted by the lights of the passing *Sombrero*.

Owing to the tropical and sub-tropical habitat, the sight of flying fish became frequent, skimming the surface for extraordinary distances, remaining aloft for maybe fifteen or twenty seconds and often for a great deal longer. Sometimes there'd be several together, pacing the ship as if competing in a whimsical steeplechase, leaping in and out of the water until they tired of their frolicking and dived to the depths of the ocean. Like so much at sea it was an amazing spectacle, of a sort completely alien to the landsman.

Shortly before their arrival at Teneriffe a caveat appeared on the ship's noticeboards, prohibiting the bringing aboard of American-made Chesterfield cigarettes. This was owing to Chesterfield - and others - being easily saleable in certain areas of Latin America where profits were temptingly huge. The worry was that if customs officials in Argentina, Brazil or Uruguay discovered any illegally imported tobacco then the company would be held responsible, while anyone caught actually selling the produce would be heavily fined and destined for a long spell in gaol.

As predicted, the *Sombrero* entered the tiny harbour at Santa Cruz as the sun was setting over Teneriffe. In so doing she passed the lilac-hulled *Pendennis Castle,* a steamer of the Union-Castle Line that was lying at anchor and transferring her passengers by tender. According to the Bosun she was one of the company's newer vessels and one that was highly regarded.

Harbour accommodation for deep-water craft at Santa Cruz was along the inner face of the harbour wall that also served as a breakwater. Apart from the *Sombrero,* a couple of inter-island ferries and a scattering of fishing boats, the only other vessel present was Blue Star's *Paraguay Star* which was homeward-bound from Buenos Aires. As for the inter-island ferries: they also connected with the Spanish mainland at Cadiz and Malaga and were generally considered a lifeline.

Until Michael said otherwise, Steve had believed the islands were named after the tiny, yellow birds that were hawked around the streets in small wooden cages or - if they were extremely fortunate - flew wild in the Teneriffe countryside. In fact, they derived their name from the Latin, *Canis,* meaning, 'Dog', as featured on the islands' coat of arms. Despite a multitude of theories no definitive reason has ever been agreed for this affiliation. However, one thing that is universally accepted is that the birds were named after the islands - an autonomous territory of Spain - and not *vice versa* as is commonly supposed.

The *Sombrero,* it transpired, would be staying in port overnight before sailing at nine in the morning. The timing seemed odd; but owing to the mail contract and the need for the minimum of delay the port authority had thoughtfully laid on a night shift. Unsurprisingly, none of her crew were complaining; although the firemen were warned that those who got sloshed and were unfit for work could expect to be severely punished - most specifically in terms of their pockets. As for Steve and his pals; the four who'd joined forces in Lisbon went ashore again together in Santa Cruz, where the Peseta was the official currency although Sterling and US Dollars were accepted.

Colin held the leadership on this occasion, promising an evening of Spanish delectation at what he reckoned was the 'most fabulous bar on the island.' However, when they arrived at this supposedly fantastic Utopia they discovered it 'out of commission', with its doors and windows firmly shuttered. However, it wasn't a complete catastrophe. It wasn't long before they were enjoying the hospitality of a neighbouring dive where the 'cerveza' flowed as freely as ever. Here they were informed that the next-door competition had been put out of business following a brawl of cataclysmic proportions. It was explained that the joint had been wrecked in the punch-up with many of the combatants hospitalized. That's typical, thought Steve, recalling a similar brawl back in Brisbane. And as for here in Teneriffe; so much for Colin's, 'most fabulous bar on the island'.

5

The six-day passage from Teneriffe to Recifé would prove to be largely uneventful. The *Sombrero* sailed as expected, slipping down the southern shores of the island towards the open Atlantic which in these more benevolent latitudes contrasted sharply with the greyness further north. Blue would be the colour from now on - until they closed the bulge of Brazil where thunderstorms were currently predicted.

In those days the package holiday industry that would eventually engulf southern Teneriffe had yet to appear, and apart from the occasional fishing village the coastline was eerily deserted. There was little to be seen in the way of greenery; rather, the shoreline resembled a moonscape whereas further north it was fertile and lush. This latter was the reason why some shipping companies, Fred Olsen in particular, maintained a regular service between the Canary Islands and London carrying cargoes of freshly-grown produce.

As the *Sombrero* headed south, towards the equator and the southern hemisphere, the temperatures soared in the 'nineties'. This was when the awning showed its worth, not only as a protective overlay but by channelling the breeze around the deck-house.

By this time a similar and much larger awning had been erected over the aftermost part of the lower promenade deck, so that passengers could lounge in the open without the fear of being barbecued. During the evenings this part of the promenade deck also served as an open-air dance floor or a venue for other entertainments - an *al fresco* cinema, for example. The film shows, which usually took place on Tuesday and Thursday evenings while the *Sombrero* was at sea, were the only occasions when crew - working stewards excepted - were allowed anywhere near the passenger accommodation unless it was an emergency, a visit to the surgery, for instance. They couldn't occupy the seats which were reserved for the passengers and off-duty officers. Instead, they perched on winches or derricks while those who were tall simply peered over everyone else. In fact, anywhere would do so long as it was behind the projector and away from the line of sight of those for whom the show was intended.

The voyage was now entering its second week, and with Michael's injuries now only a minor impediment there was a feeling of cosy contentment. One thing was for sure; when everything ran smoothly it was noticeably less stressful in the *Sombrero's* crew galley than it ever could be in a passenger ship pantry. They were seldom bothered: in fact, the only time they clapped eyes an officer was in the course of the morning inspection. Okay, there was the occasional grouse about the food - mostly from the same bunch of whingers - but it was largely good natured with no malice meant so no-one was badly put out. Michael gave as good as he got and life drifted onwards serenely.

It was while crossing the Atlantic, during one of their quieter interludes, when he and Michael were chatting about everything and nothing, that Steve discovered more than he'd bargained for. You see, Michael's life was a wide-open book, as if he hadn't a secret worth hiding. He told about his youth in the far west of Ireland; how he'd grown up in a hamlet on the coast; how as a teenager he'd gone away to sea as there little work to be had nearer home; and how, during a spell of leave he'd met a beauty called Clodagh Maguire.

Apparently, he'd fallen head-over-heels in love and before a fortnight was out he'd proposed. Now then, Clodagh was devoutly

Catholic, and she'd made it clear from the start there'd be no hanky-panky of any description until the wedding ceremony was over - that's assuming she accepted his proposal. As it happened, she'd no intention of refusing because she was smitten with the idea of a home of her own, a man about the house and all the other things enamoured girls dream of. Her parents seemed to approve so that wasn't a problem; so before Michael returned to his ship she accepted - on condition that he leave the sea and apply for a vacancy on their doorstep. Michael, besotted to say the least, did as he was bade, secured the job in a local hotel and they were married as soon as was practical, setting up home in a small rented cottage in Sligo.

The marriage had lasted less than a week. Clodagh, you see, was frigid - totally unresponsive; and that was no good to a red-blooded boyo like Michael who'd played by the rules but now expected his rewards. But Clodagh was having none of it. She'd got what she wanted; a man to show off to her friends and a snug little house she could boast of. Michael in return would get his laundry and the housework attended to and that was about all he could count on. And that - to put it mildly - had been her downfall. To use words of his own Michael had gone out on the piss; had finally arrived home full of Guinness; had smashed up the cottage, scaring the shit out of Clodagh; and stormed out of the house wearing only the clothes he stood up in. The following day he'd returned to find Clodagh had hopped it; so, he'd packed a bag, collected his discharge book and hadn't seen hide of her since.

'Sounds like an intriguing leave,' remarked Steve, philosophically, after Michael had recounted his tale with Whisky asleep on his lap, cat-napping through the trauma of a couple's entire married life. 'Do you ever hear anything from her?'

'Not a dicky bird,' answered Michael, sucking on a chunk of pineapple that had formed part of the dinner time pudding, 'and that doesn't bother me either - and you know what? I haven't even been back to Ireland. Still, it happened a long time ago. I eventually got hooked up with Vera and - well, you know what happened. We kept in touch and continued to meet whenever, although I was still only a client in those days. But now it's got to the stage where we live together, at least when I fetch up in London.'

There were other occasions, in the warm tropical evenings, at that favourite gathering place, the hatch cover in the after well-deck, when Ambrose Richardson, a gigantic Trinidadian fireman, kept his audience enthralled with tales of his years at sea and at home in the sunny Caribbean. Ambrose was vitality personified and no one, it seemed, could resist his enthusiasm for life.

With regard to ethnic diversity: it was a feature of the *Sombrero* that her crew was largely cosmopolitan, with in addition to the aforementioned stewards, individuals from Australia, Malta, Norway and as the presence of Ambrose indicated, the West Indies. This was in addition, of course, to the usual diaspora of Scots, Ulstermen and Welsh, not to mention the English and those from the Irish Republic. Whatever, thus far, with the occasional blip they all seemed to gel and there'd been little to upset the apple cart.

One morning, during a quieter spell when Steve and the Donkeyman were idling, they spotted another vessel low on the horizon, an unlikely event given the ocean's immensity. Way out here, in the middle of a watery wilderness, if you saw another ship at all it was usually at night and even then it was often just a glimmer. So, what was the purpose of this 'stranger', a smudge in the distance only a minute or so ago but which was now converging with the *Sombrero*. Others joined them at the rail; and speculation was rife, until the other ship closed and they espied the device on her funnel.

'Ahhh! it's the *Poncho,* announced the Donkeyman, his subsequent words being completely drowned out by a blast from the *Sombrero's* siren. This sounding of sirens - the *Poncho* was being equally as raucous - continued for a good fifteen seconds before silence resumed and the Donkeyman's words could be deciphered. 'She's homeward bound with a cargo of chilled beef and offal, nearly all of it from The Argentine and Uruguay. It's a nice little number on them ships,' he added, nodding at the *Poncho* which was now receding astern on her way home to Europe and London. 'They don't carry passengers but call at the same ports that we do, as well as Le Havre and Rotterdam.' He also explained that whenever ships of the same company were in the same stretch of ocean they'd pass as close to each other as possible, and that the sounding of sirens was a greeting.

But these isolated occurrences apart, as far as Steve was concerned it was generally a case of routine: turn to in the morning; rake out and make up the fire; collect the stores; peel the potatoes; help cook the breakfast before eating himself - and this after everyone else. It was very much the same throughout the rest of the day with little in the way of variation.

If the truth were known, of all the chores that formed part of his role then strapping up was the most disagreeable. In fact, it was the only task that he had to perform that was more onerous than its pantry equivalent, where crockery and such could be quickly polished off whereas utensils and pans proved the opposite. You see, there was no such substance as 'Teflon', the solid remains of many a dish clinging on to the metal like a clam. Wire-wool was invariably the answer, along with 'Ajax' and a 'tool'; maybe a serving spoon or a fish slice that functioned as a surrogate chisel. The effects of the scouring showed clearly on the aluminium pans; similarly on the roasting trays, that dazzled like mirrors when new but soon became lustreless and dull. As for the scrub-out; that was a breeze thanks to sugi and a stiff-bristled broom.

For his part Michael was behaving, drinking only his weekly allowance, a case of either Tennant's or Tuborg which each contained two-dozen cans. His redeeming feature was that instead of embarking on a bender - his previous practice - he'd settle for three cans a session. There were even instances when he'd gift one to Steve who owing to his junior status couldn't purchase alcohol - at least aboard ship; although rather bizarrely he could obtain it at will when ashore.

It was at about this time that Steve became aware of an irritation, mostly around his groin and armpits; and while a cursory inspection showed only a slight inflammation, closer examination revealed - lice. To be more specific they were crabs, which were lice of a sort and certainly no less horrific. He'd been considering a visit to the surgery, for possible diagnosis and medication, but that was now out of the question. Further embarrassment was the last thing he needed; and so, he sought a reason for the plague and more especially an effective self-treatment. The first part of the equation seemed simple. His bed was clean, he dhobied regularly and showered as frequently as anyone so what on earth could have caused the contagion? He didn't associate with dodgy women so the answer was most certainly - wool. That must be it, he thought, as he scratched like a flea-ridden mongrel; that deck cargo of wool aboard the *Alice Springs* that he and Peter had slept in. Instead of being comfy and snug the stuff had been filthy while smelling of the animals that had worn it. Consequently, contact with the wool had been relatively brief but it was doubtless the cause of his lodgers.

So, how to effect a safe remedy? He'd heard of how some had dislodged them with a knife while others had used a lighted cigarette. However, neither of these treatments appealed; not least because they'd obviously be painful but success couldn't be guaranteed. Then, out of the blue he had a brainwave. He suddenly recalled seeing a can of insecticide in the locker adjacent to the fridge. He could hardly believe his luck, his reasoning being that if it exterminated flies then it ought to eradicate crabs. When all was said and done, they were each a variety of insect. He couldn't imagine a physician prescribing a course of insecticide as a cure for bodily infestation; but there was nothing to lose so he'd try it and chance the reaction. Grabbing the aerosol while Michael wasn't looking he made a dash for the heads with the excuse that he had to use the loo. Now then, the use of a fly-spray may have been risky but it proved to be highly successful. Within a matter of hours the crabs had disappeared and with them an awful lot of woe.

That very same night there was rain - and it rained with an astonishing intensity. Steve had never seen anything like it - raindrops as big as shilling pieces, drenching anyone who hadn't an oilskin; meaning anyone who wasn't a member of the deck department but who still had to venture outside. This, of course, included Michael and himself who lived amidships but whose workplace was high on the poop. It meant they were soaked by the time they arrived, the only up-side being that with the temperature still in the eighties - along with the heat from the stove - it didn't take long to dry out. Conversely, he was no sooner dry then Steve had to dash to the stores. By the time he returned both he and the stores were as waterlogged as the current spell of weather.

Whisky didn't like the rain either. He refused to leave the shelter of the awning, looking forlornly at Michael and Steve, as much as to ask, "Why don't you stop it raining?" And when it became clear that they couldn't he just moped, as close as he could to the galley without actually moving inside.

It wasn't just the heaviness of the rain so much as its very persistence. It just didn't stop, for the best part of forty-eight hours. It thudded on the awning that until only yesterday had been a shield against ultra-violet rays. But not only that: in the oppressive, saturated atmosphere the exhaust from the *Sombrero's* funnels beat down on her decks and living areas, filtering through the awning that until very recently had shrouded a fresh-air oasis. The same applied to the smoke from the galley chimney. It drifted inside and out; in fact, in every direction except upwards.

And then came the thunder and lightning, crashing and flashing and rumbling for hours without any sign of it easing. At the first clap of thunder the cat disappeared, out of harm's way beneath a locker. No amount of coaxing could persuade him to emerge and he stayed there until the storm fizzled out. Consequently, he missed an exhibition of St Elmo's Fire, a blue-tinged, fluorescent enigma that danced around the aerials and rigging, a symptom of the electrically-charged atmosphere. But the display was transient and Steve had to ask if what he'd witnessed had actually occurred. Michael assured him that it had; and thus, another fine spectacle could be safely consigned to his intellect.

Then, out of the blue, early one gloomy afternoon and shortly before their arrival at Recifé, the rain ceased as abruptly as it had started. The sky remained sullen with overcast and the atmosphere heavy but visibility was greatly improved.

Their estimated arrival time was reportedly between four and four-thirty so landfall could be expected as imminent. Armed with this info Steve began scouring the horizon, eager for his first ever glimpse of the fifth largest country on earth. But the skyline remained stubbornly empty; and it remained so until, suddenly - and indistinctly - away to the south-west, there arose three columns of smoke. He initially thought that the smoke was a patch of thicker cloud until its source was eventually revealed. Three chimneys grew out of the ocean - followed by the coast of Brazil.

By late afternoon the *Sombrero* was tied up in Recifé, a city so named from the hidden off-shore reefs that protected its harbour and coastline. One of the largest conurbations on the continent it was also capital of the north-eastern state of Pernambuco.

The immediate port area was typical, with cranes, transit sheds, a maze or railway tracks and all the other dockside paraphernalia - but what lay beyond was a mystery. Steve had heard all sorts of tales about Recifé - but a lot of it may well have been fiction. His first impression was that it was just another port - albeit a port with a racy reputation. Well, he thought, there's only one way to find out; and so, finishing work as he did well ahead of his chums he proceeded ashore, having arranged to meet up with them later.

The road from the port was rutted and potholed while the pavements were dusty and broken. Wharves and warehouses, many of them with crumbling brickwork, flanked the seaward side of the street while along the other stretched a row of wooden huts. The huts - unmistakeably dwellings - each had a pretty front garden encircled by a rickety fence. Steve's initial assumption was that these must be the homes of dock workers, and the women who were nattering over one of the fences were probably dock workers' wives. It all seemed a little dilapidated. But that was only to be expected, he supposed, given the nature of the area; and that Brazil was renowned for its extremes with some of its citizens being outrageously rich while the majority were desperately poor. He also noted that the women were black; most likely the descendants of African slaves who were shipped to Brazil in the seventeenth and eighteenth centuries to toil in the sugar-cane industry on which Pernambuco had flourished.

This brought to mind a story that Ambrose Richardson had related, about West Indian dockers who were engaged in the handling of sugar. Steve had been shovelling the commodity into his coffee when Ambrose had interrupted, 'You wouldn't be doing that if you knew what I know.'

'Why? What do you know that I don't?' Steve had retorted, half guessing that Ambrose wasn't joking. 'I'm only putting sugar in my coffee.'

'Well,' Ambrose had replied, 'I was watching these dockers back in Bridgetown, trimming sugar in the holds of a tramp. They were down there from sun-up till teatime and not one of them came up for a pee.' Ambrose had then winked, tapping the tip of his nose with an index finger.

Steve had looked first at his coffee and then at Ambrose before emptying his mug down the sink. Ambrose meanwhile had departed, chuckling softly as Steve made another mug of coffee, this one without any sugar.

The evening was sultry and warm causing Steve to perspire, much as he had over the previous fortnight and would do for at least another month. He mopped the sweat from his brow as he walked - until the suspicion arose that he was being followed. He swung around and there, only a few feet behind him, was one of the women who'd been cheerfully chatting with her 'neighbour'.

The woman, who was as black as a crow, built like a tank and a potential heavyweight boxing champion, stopped in her tracks, smiled a huge beaming smile, and asked, 'You wanna go jig-a-jig, Johnny?' And then, without waiting for an astonished Steve to reply she took hold of his arm and wrapped it - as far as it would extend - around her ample forty-inch waist, adding brazenly, 'I'll give you the time of your life.'

Steve was gob-smacked. He looked first at the woman and then back at the huts, suddenly realizing that she was a prostitute and that the huts formed one of the brothel communities for which Recifé was notorious. His mind flashed back to the 'Vindi', and the lecture concerning the perils of tropical and sexually-transmitted diseases that a visiting doctor had so graphically illustrated. In a state of alarm he unwrapped the arm, stammering, 'No Cruzeiros. No Cruzeiros,' - which was the god's honest truth given that he hadn't had chance to change any of his sterling into the Brazilian currency - before turning on his heel and fleeing, leaving his would-be wooer hurling a string of abuse while awaiting more willing clientele.

'Christ! That was a close call,' he told himself, as his heart-rate lessened, the unexpected encounter causing him to perspire even more freely in this city just south of the equator. 'Start messing around with women like that and you'll end up with a dick like a salami.'

Away from the docks the city was attractive if frayed. It abounded with glorious Portuguese colonial architecture in innumerable hues whilst the sound of music reverberated - issuing forth from doorways and windows. These were the rhythms of Brazil that up until then Steve had heard only on the wireless, courtesy of the BBC, most probably on 'Housewife's Choice'. And as for the extremes of colour; they even extended to the skins of the local inhabitants, ranging from black through to white with countless shades of tan in between.

The bars were teeming, with girls on the game, couples swaying and men getting sozzled in the heat. Steve eventually met up with his pals and they joined with the throng, finally arriving back at the *Sombrero* in the early hours - although apart from his brush with the prostitute his mind was a stupefied blank.

6

Four hours sleep did them no good at all and Steve was left nursing a 'blinder'. Michael by comparison was as fit as a fiddle despite - according to one account - having demolished a bottle of cachaça, a locally-produced head-slammer that was distilled from sugar-cane whilst lacking the purity of rum. Cachaça was what Steve had been drinking; neat, as it was meant to be, provided you were aware of the pitfalls. Steve hadn't been aware and now he was paying for his folly.

'Here, get that down you,' said Michael, handing him a tumblerful of water with another one waiting in the wings. 'You're dehydrated - that's why you feel so bloody awful. Next time you sample the cachaça be sure to drink plenty of water - then you'll feel fine in the morning.'

'Thanks for the advice,' mumbled Steve, ungratefully, before downing the water and sloping off in search of some codeine, 'it's a pity you didn't mention it yesterday.' And as for drinking plenty of water as a hangover remedy: he seemed to remember that from somewhere - and he'd have to remember it in future.

The *Sombrero* sailed mid-morning - heading for Rio, a run of over nine-hundred miles; or in nautical parlance, a smidgen over a couple of days steaming. These runs between ports down the Brazilian coast seldom took longer and before the morning was out, thanks to the water and codeine, Steve was keenly anticipating their arrival at what was probably the most evocatively-named city in the Americas - with the exception perhaps of Buenos Aires.

Steve had long since discovered that life at sea was never ever short of surprises and that there was always distraction of some sort; and this was the case after dinner when a camouflaged spider as big as a saucer was seen sunning itself on a hatch cover. The part-cargo loaded at Recifé had included a consignment of bananas, the probable source of the arachnid given its analogous yellow and black colouring. Whatever, it attracted an audience with some of those present admiring its tincture while most thought it probably poisonous. However, all this was made rapidly irrelevant, courtesy of a callous EDH. The fellow, who was obviously a philistine and definitely a moron, pushed through the crowd, removed a shoe; and using the heel as a hammer, brutally obliterated the spider. There were cries of dismay with the culprit being threatened with a lynching - and it was easy to understand the sentiment. Everyone knew that the creature might bite but killing it was zoological vandalism.

In January 1501, when a Portuguese expedition entered an inlet from the sea while exploring the coast of Brazil they imagined they'd discovered an estuary; so given the month of the year they christened it Rio de Janeiro. That the inlet was actually a vast natural harbour appears to have been overlooked. 'River of January' it remained while the associated settlement evolved as the 'Rio' of today.

The harbour at Rio is spectacular, surrounded as it is by precipitous mountains that sweep down to the island-speckled sea. Add to all this the luxuriant greenery, not forgetting the stupendous beaches at Copacabana and Ipanema, and It's easy to see why the location is so romantically exotic. Michael took it all in his stride but Steve was agog, hardly able to believe that he was witnessing something exquisite.

It was past the beaches that the *Sombrero* made her cautious approach, passing the legendary Sugar Loaf Mountain before a broad sweeping turn brought her close to the naval base and several former Royal Navy warships. Then there was the airport, at the water's edge; and a Dakota airliner soaring high overhead before climbing over Sugar Loaf Mountain. And there, beyond and above all, loomed the massif of Mount Corcavado. But it wasn't so much the mountain as the statue at its peak that was eye catching. It was Christ the Redeemer himself, head in the clouds and arms outstretched as he kept vigil over the city at his feet.

The *Sombrero* tied up in virtually the heart of the metropolis, directly astern of an American liner that was disgorging her gaudily-dressed tourists. The antithesis of the stately *Sombrero* the American vessel - a Moore-McCormack liner - was hugely futuristic with a streamlined superstructure and a funnel that was strikingly sham, her exhaust being expelled through twin uptakes aft, immediately abaft her promenade decks. However, the make-believe funnel did serve a purpose by incorporating a solarium and an expensively-furnished observation lounge. She was in fact the fifteen-thousand ton *Argentina,* which, along with her sister *Brasil,* maintained a service between New York and Buenos Aires.

Moore-McCormack weren't the only American company plying this eastern seaboard as following a similar route were the steamers *Del Mar, Del Norte* and *Del Sud.* Belonging to the Louisiana-based Delta Line these stylish passenger-cargo liners were also distinctive in having large, dummy funnels with twin uptakes aft taking the exhaust gasses clear of the ships. The seven-week trip to Buenos Aires and return both commenced and terminated at New Orleans on the Mississippi delta.

From his handily-placed lookout Steve watched bemused as the *Argentina's* 'bloods' disembarked, pockets full of Dollars that would doubtless be exchanged for all manner of trinkets and trifles. The sight of wealthy Americans, along with the adjacent ritzy neighbourhood, could easily have suggested that Rio was a city of plenty and that no-one survived on the breadline, but as Michael pointed out, nothing could have been further from the truth. He explained that what appeared to be affluent suburbs, stretching away up the hillsides, were in fact the infamous 'Favelas', erected using whatever materials were at hand by those who would otherwise be homeless. Nor did it follow that the inhabitants were out-of-work layabouts - far from it. In fact, they probably toiled harder than most, with many eking a living from the municipal dumps, salvaging anything they could gainfully sell.

Notwithstanding, as Steve was shortly to discover; the Cariocas - Rio's citizens - were a smiling collective of exuberance and to share in their company was a joy. He eventually went ashore after dinner, mixing with the crowds, exploring gardens and parks - and avenues so wide that eight lanes of traffic were commonplace. He found the gardens an explosion of colour; while the air was alive with butterflies and birds carrying hues as varied as the rainbow.

And then there were the shops and street-vendors, all apparently competing with identical or similar merchandise. Colourful clothing and decorative guitars were just some of the items for sale; while among the most popular purchases were butterfly trays - essentially tea trays - intricately adorned with the wings of the most beautiful species. They sold by the cartload; but Steve couldn't help wondering at the ethics that allowed such magnificent creatures to be caught and slaughtered for a relative handful of Cruzeiros. He was tempted, but his conscience kept his cash in his pocket. Instead he bought a showy guitar, something he couldn't play but felt sure he'd be able to master. He later discovered that in Brazil the killing of butterflies for adornment was illegal and had been for a good many years. Rather, the wings on the trays that were currently being sold had been harvested from already dead insects. And so it was that he made his way back to the *Sombrero*, guitar slung over his shoulder while humming the first few bars of Duane Eddy's 'Shazam', an instrumental gem that he'd practise at later that evening.

The visit to Rio had been short but had transcended all expectations; an impossible dream that had happily come true thanks wholly to a passion for the sea. Unfortunately the moment had passed and later that evening, with the shoreline resplendent, the *Sombrero* effected her departure. Heading out into the South Atlantic she safely negotiated the Tijucas Rocks that thirteen years earlier had overseen the *Magdalena's* demise. Her next port of call would be Santos - and it had an awful lot to live up to.

Back in their cabin there was a jam session; if a couple of guitars - one of them appallingly strummed - and some cacophonous vocals were worthy of such a description. To be fair, Alan was a proficient guitarist, sufficiently talented to provide a useful enough backing to the vocal contortions of his room-mates. Steve, by comparison, was crap, something that was patently obvious; although by the end of the evening he could pick out a tune that the others could just about recognize.

7

There could be little doubt as the *Sombrero* headed south that Steve was doing most of the cooking; part of his tuition according to Michael who was becoming increasingly scarce. The disappearances were supposedly to discuss menu options with the Chef, although it soon became clear that he was sharing a tot with his cronies. Steve wasn't fooled; but surprisingly, neither was he unduly perturbed. In fact, he positively enjoyed being left all alone with Whisky as his only companion. That said, Michael wasn't entirely negligent and occasionally popped up, if only to keep an eye on Steve's progress.

In many respects Michael was his own worst enemy as the crew were quick to remind him. You see, Steve was nothing if not creative - developing his own specialities, the most unlikely being mashed potato. It may have been the extra cup of milk or the additional dollop of butter; but whatever, Steve's mashed potato always possessed a creamier, more smoother quality that the sailors and firemen appreciated. Consequently, Michael was frequently taunted with, "Let the youngster mash the spuds."

As for personal hygiene: Steve was fortunate in having plenty of clothing so dhobying was off his agenda - at least when in port where it was allowed to accumulate, being attended to when they were at sea. And so, having the run of the galley that's where performed his laundry; on the stove, after hours, when it boiled in a bucket before being rinsed and dried beneath the awning. There was only one snag and it involved the support in his underpants. Excessive boiling caused the elastic to perish and they ended up sagging around his knees.

Other crew-members experienced similar mishaps, such as happened to the Assistant Cook. On this particular evening Steve was nodding off when he - along with the rest of the working alleyway - was startled awake by a spiralling crescendo of cackling. With most of the doors on their hooks it was impossible not to be heard and the occupants were quick to investigate. They didn't have too far to look for at the end of the alleyway, near the main galley entrance, stood Lenny who was creased up with laughter. Lenny was an excitable fellow whose hysterical laugh would have done credit to a horror movie soundtrack. The tears were rolling down his cheeks as he held up a shirt that was shrivelled and hideously shrunken. 'What the hell have you done?' asked Colin, staring first at Lenny and then at the shirt that wasn't much larger than a handkerchief.

'Stupid bastard. The fuckin' shirt's made of nylon and he's only been and boiled it on the stove?' answered Derek, shaking his head while gazing at Lenny in despair. 'But not only that, the silly sod forgot all about it and it's been boiling since soon after dinner.' Upon Derek's pronouncement Lenny's laughter attained even higher frequencies; and became so infectious that before very long the entire assemblage was in stitches. When the excitement eventually subsided and Lenny had wandered off, clutching his shirt and still giggling inanely, Derek added, 'I told him to let the Laundryman do it but he wouldn't listen. Reckoned at twenty fags a throw it'd be cheaper to buy a new shirt.'

However, trusting one's laundry to the Laundryman wasn't without hazards of its own as the Second Steward was soon to discover. He'd handed a uniform shirt to this worthy with instructions for it to be laundered and ironed. Unfortunately, while the chain-smoking Laundryman was carrying out the ironing a flake of lighted ash fell from the tip of his cigarette. It burnt a hole in the shirt and rendered it not fit for purpose. The Second Steward, who despite his position could swear like a fishwife, immediately went on the warpath. 'You fuckin' eejit,' he stormed, holding up the garment to examine the damage which was even worse than he'd originally feared, 'you're not fit to be in charge of a shithouse let alone a passenger-ship laundry. Well! You can fuckin' well buy me a new one. I'll take it out of slops, charge it to your account - and you can forget about that packet of Players.'

Santos, the largest port in Latin America, served the mushrooming city of Sao Paulo which lay about fifty miles inland. It possessed none of the grandeur of Rio, being mainly industrial while lacking any natural attraction. However, it wasn't without its appeal, most notably a magnificent seafront that at over three miles long and embroidered with gardens, was strung around a gently-curving bay. Their approach was through a long, narrow channel, between the mainland and several large islands that conveniently served as a breakwater. The *Sombrero* arrived around sun-up and wouldn't be sailing until midnight, giving ample opportunity for an afternoon ashore and again - more enticingly - later.

As soon as the *Sombrero* was secured a wheezing steam locomotive of Edwardian vintage shunted a long rake of vans alongside. The contents were deposited on the quayside - in itself not unusual: what was unusual was that the cargo was loaded without being checked by either dockworker, tally-man or seaman. Comprising mostly agricultural produce it was bound for the cities further south, as was almost everything else that had been shipped on their way down the coast.

As viewed from the *Sombrero* the seafront had stirred the imagination; and so, straight after dinner with Alan for company Steve set a course for the beach. Michael had mentioned that in view of the distance they'd be well-advised to take the tram. With only two hours to spare the suggestion made sense so they headed for the nearest tram stop.

Although neither of them knew it, by choosing the tram they'd embraced one of life's great adventures. For a start they couldn't speak the language so couldn't ask directions to the tram stop. And then, once they'd found a stop they'd no way of knowing if the tram they were waiting for would take them to their intended destination. As for asking others in the queue: that proved equally as fruitless until a passing pedestrian, a distinguished old gentleman with a flowing white beard - who also happened to have a good grasp of English - advised that each and every tram from that particular stop would be heading in the direction of the seafront.

And so they waited - and they waited, the queue growing longer by the second until, quite unexpectedly, a rattling old 'toast-rack' came swinging around a corner and squealed to a halt at the pavement. Steve knew all there was to know about toast racks - open-sided trams that had acquired their nickname owing to the upright seating arrangements. But at least it was transport, the only trouble being that the contraption was packed, with passengers even riding on the running-boards. It seemed impossible; and the boys were on the verge of giving up - until the queue leapt aboard prompting them to follow suit while grasping for any free handhold. And then the tram rattled off, lurching and swaying while those on the outside - Steve and Alan included - clung on as if their lives depended on it. The journey was nothing if not exhilarating, broken only when they paused at a stop, or when the driver - using a long slender pole - leant from his cab to switch the points. Surprising no-one fell off, not even the conductor who, with the agility of a monkey, collected his fares by clambering inside and out and around those who were riding on the running-board. Amazingly, he performed his acrobatics with coins gripped tightly between his knuckles. Apparently, he carried the money in the fashion described to avoid having to rummage for change. Steve paid his fare as he hung from a rail, using his free hand to forage for cash. Sensibly, Alan had his fare already sorted, a lesson that was clearly worth learning.

The seafront at Santos proved every bit as splendid as the view from the *Sombrero* had promised. There was a tree-lined esplanade with well-tended flowerbeds all accessed from a broad and busy boulevard. Cafés and bars lined the opposite side of the street along with apartment blocks, hotels and shops. Ice cream kiosks completed the picture which unlike at home was devoid of seaside amusements.

The boys bought ice cream and sat beneath the trees watching lizards as they scurried through the sand. Meanwhile, youngsters played soccer on the beach, pretending they were Pelé, the World Cup-winning legend who played domestically for Santos. They considered going for a swim but thought better of it, not knowing if sharks were indigenous. Instead they became amateur photographers, snapping away with their brownies before time called a halt, bringing their brief excursion to a close. Their return to the *Sombrero* was equally as fraught as the outward journey, the overcrowded tram being even more crammed than its predecessor. On this occasion a teenager with the qualities of a tennis ball did fall off, tumbling through the dust before he picked himself up and began chasing the tram like a greyhound.

An evening ashore in Santos meant a trawl of the dockside 'attractions'. As expected these establishments were bawdy and gaudy but Utopia for seamen with money, few showing interest in the more salubrious attractions such as those that were closer to the seafront. Of all the watering holes on this neon-lit enclave the most popular was the Bar Americano. It was probably owing to this particular dive being further up-market than its rivals, the management boasting that they employed the prettiest girls; charged the lowest prices; gave exemplary service; and that the

74

customer received greater exchange for his American Dollars than anywhere else in Santos. Whether or not it was as generous with Sterling was debatable, but it was readily accepted and there was little if any complaint.

Whatever, the *Sombrero's* firemen certainly capitalized, delaying her departure by several hours while sufficient were rounded up to man the ship. In the event only one was left behind while his shipmates could expect retribution. She sailed in the hour before daybreak, while Steve and his chums were still sleeping off the evening's extravagance.

8

The run to the River Plate - which is actually an estuary for numerous other rivers - was largely without incident with only a couple of exceptions, one of them highly amusing while the other was a matter of routine. The first involved Colin and Jim who were emptying the main galley rosie, which wasn't quite as simple it sounds.

A rosie, the wire-handled, five-gallon oil drum that sufficed aboard most British cargo ships, was usually easily transported - provided it wasn't full of liquid. It was simply a matter of hoisting it to the chute and tipping it, the rubbish plopping either into the sea; or if in port, the barge that was moored alongside. Alternatively, a modern, state-of-the-art passenger liner might be equipped with a garbage-disposal system that could be activated by the flick of a switch. However, owing to her age, her intermediate size and a lack of investment the rosie in the *Sombrero's* main galley was an over-sized galvanized dustbin that was the devil's own job to mobilize.

Steve was a spectator on this particular afternoon as Colin and Jim performed miracles. Somehow, they'd manoeuvred their dustbin on to the after well-deck having dragged it the length of the working alleyway. That, however, had been the easy bit. They were now faced with the task of raising it to the chute that was attached to the starboard bulwark. It didn't help that the contents were semi-fluid, not only increasing its weight but giving it a degree of independence. Still, they weren't to be thwarted and with an effort supreme they hoisted it up, their intention being to roll it to the chute where the contents could be safely jettisoned. But the bin was determined to frustrate them. It wobbled and rolled, backwards and forwards as its custodians fought to control it. As sod's law dictated, instead of rolling inboard and spilling its contents it lurched egotistically outboard, out of their grasp before plummeting headlong overboard. It hit the sea with a smack sending spray flying high before sinking to the depths of the Atlantic. The lads looked first at the water where the bin had disappeared and then at each other before exploding with laughter, enjoying the moment as a prelude to facing the music.

It later emerged that Frederico Henrique, normally mild-mannered and not disposed to histrionics, hadn't been amused and had let fly with both barrels blazing. He'd then tasked the delinquents with securing a replacement before significant rubbish accumulated. Salvation had arrived in the form of the Donkeyman who'd furnished a fifty-gallon oil drum, complete with a pair of rope handles. He'd also advised that owing to the oil drum's capacity - which was considerably in excess of that of the ill-fated dustbin - it shouldn't be unduly overloaded. The oil drum was eventually accepted although the Chef wasn't entirely impressed - notwithstanding his previous infatuation with a dustbin.

The second and more workaday eventuality involved the issuing of visas. Before anyone was allowed ashore in Buenos Aires they had to be in possession of a visa which - for those without one - was prepared during the course of the voyage. Shortly after their departure from Teneriffe the Writer had taken Steve's photograph which after it had been developed, was pasted into an Argentine visa card. The card, which contained his personal details including his fingerprints, had to be carried whenever he was ashore. The completed documents were distributed on the morning of their arrival at Montevideo.

Prior to their arrival at Montevideo, Steve had been keeping his eyes peeled for the wreck of the *Admiral Graf Spee,* the German pocket battleship which had been scuttled off the port following what the British would later term, the 'Battle of the River Plate'. It was the first major sea battle of the Second World War; but prior to that the raider had wrought havoc among British and allied merchant shipping in the Indian and South Atlantic Oceans. Her destruction became a priority; and she was eventually sighted and engaged by three British warships, the heavy cruiser *HMS Exeter* and the light cruisers *Achilles* and *Ajax.* In the course of the ensuing action the *Exeter* was crippled while the *Admiral Graf Spee* was badly damaged, to such an extent that she sought refuge in Montevideo, capital of Uruguay, a nation that was nominally 'neutral' but known to be strongly pro-British. The Uruguayans granted the German ship sanctuary - allowing her to bury her dead and obtain medical attention for her wounded - but only for seventy-two hours owing to the restrictions imposed by international neutrality legislation. Rather than sail and allow his ship to be destroyed by what he believed to be superior British forces - falsely reported as massing off the River Plate estuary - the *Admiral Graf Spees's* commander, Captain Hans Langsdorff, decided this wasn't an option. His vessel was subsequently scuttled in the approaches to Montevideo, her crew being interned for the duration. This didn't include Captain Langsdorff who adopted the 'honourable' exit, courtesy of his own revolver.

'You can stare all you like but you won't see anything,' said Michael, joining Steve at the rail now that tea was finished and there was an evening ashore to look forward to. 'She was broken up ages ago - by Argentine scrap merchants, apparently.'

'Not all of her, it wasn't,' chipped in the Bosun, who'd sidled up beside them and had been silently eavesdropping. 'It's reckoned there's still a load of her down there, waiting to be salvaged - but Michael's right about one thing. You won't be able to see anything. But that,' he added, turning and extending an arm over Steve's shoulder and indicating in the direction of Argentina which was miles away over the horizon, 'is a different matter.' Steve followed the finger and was amazed by the sight a liner lying high on a sandbank. 'She's the old *Highland Chieftain,'* continued the Bosun, firing up a Capstan and coughing. 'She was sold out of the Royal Mail fleet a couple of years ago, after the *Amazon* had been delivered. She was bought by a Gibraltar-based whaling concern who intending using her as a depot ship but the 'Chieftain' wasn't playing by the rules. The *Calpean Star,* as she was by this time, was on her way out of Buenos Aires when she suffered a problem with her steering gear. She was taken in tow but an engine room explosion was the final nail in her coffin and she's been lying on the sand ever since.'

'That's right,' agreed Michael, who was also studying the former Royal Mail liner which he'd sailed in several years earlier, 'and a sandbank's the best place for her. Fourteen to a cabin we were - in the 'Glory Hole' - crammed in like bloody sardines, but, it's sad to see her looking so desolate.'

The Bosun agreed. 'Too right - but she's still manned, mind you, by a couple of watchmen who maintain her lights as a warning for others to stand clear.'

Other than in newsreels and photos Steve had never seen a proper ship wreck and the sight of the old *Highland Chieftain* sitting high and dry like a beached leviathan was not only depressing but a reminder of the perils of seafaring. He was to discover that like the Goodwin Sands the River Plate was a maritime graveyard that in the following decade would host a peacetime tragedy of terrifying wartime magnitude.

Montevideo transpired as being pleasantly aloof, and although there were the expected inequalities there was none of the obvious poverty that had sullied the ports of Brazil. Indeed, along with Argentina, Uruguay could boast some of the highest living standards on the continent, despite economic problems caused chiefly by inflation and a ridiculously benevolent welfare system. It may sound utterly bizarre but it was widely reported - although not verified - that a Uruguayan labourer could retire on a full state pension at the age of fifty-five, ten years earlier than his British counterpart. But whatever: the streets were clean and well maintained; there was clearly a rich heritage that seamlessly interacted with a vibrant social scene; while importantly for people like Steve, there was none of the lunatic driving that in most of South America made pedestrian survival a lottery.

Being geographically adjacent there were extremely close ties between this delightful little country and The Argentine, her larger and more flamboyant neighbour. Regular ferry sailings linked Montevideo with Buenos Aires, the vessels maintaining the service being the *Ciudad de Montevideo* and the *Ciudad de Buenos Aires.* However, the trip along the winding channels of the River Plate was time consuming, so for those in a hurry and possessing the wherewithal, a flying-boat proved the solution. These aircraft, which were extremely popular among those who could afford them, operated between the harbour at Montevideo and the river at Buenos Aires.

For a change, Steve went ashore on his own, ignoring the bars and cafés, preferring instead to hang on to his cash so as to supplement his sub in Argentina. Instead, he gained an object lesson in how to enjoy fresh surroundings without spending vast sums of money. He strolled and he stared and he sat and he watched, observing how others conducted themselves. It was a revelation; and by the end of the evening he'd already decided that henceforth, wherever he went, in addition to living the high life, he'd indulge in some cultural activity.

But aboard the *Sombrero* - regardless of Montevideo's attractions - there was hardly a soul who didn't prefer Buenos Aires where the night-life was reputedly unrivalled. Some had remarked that it was no longer so lively and exciting, the latest government having gone to extraordinary lengths to eradicate prostitution. On the other hand, those more discerning had said it didn't matter anyway as the girls were still there and it was simply a matter of locating them. Steve wasn't bothered as he wasn't the least bit interested in prostitutes; and anyway, given the volatile nature of Argentine politics there was always the chance that by the time they arrived the present regime would have been overthrown and been replaced by yet another, more tolerant administration. Whatever, sometime during the following twenty-four hours he'd discover for himself what the Argentine capital had to offer; and of one thing he was certain - he wouldn't be hugely disappointed.

On a morning of mist the *Sombrero* made her way up the estuary, her estimated arrival in 'The City of Fine Airs' being somewhere in the region of noon. The River Plate - translated from the Spanish, 'Rio de la Plata', meaning 'River of Silver' - looked anything but. The water had the colour of mustard, laden as it was with silt washed down from the hinterland via the tributaries that formed the Plate delta. Indeed, the accumulation of silt was the principal reason for the *Sombrero's* meandering progress, with shipping duty-bound to adhere to the clearly-buoyed channel.

The Punta Indio Channel, which has its origins south of the port of Montevideo, winds into the Banco Chico Channel which in turn twists up to Buenos Aires. At various locations upperworks protruded from the water, marking the final resting places of steamers that had strayed from the fairway.

The rivers that drain into the estuary originate on the Argentine side of the Andes, in the Bolivian mountains, the Brazilian jungles and in the lowlands of Paraguay and Uruguay. The rivers Paraná, Paraguay and Uruguay are just three of those that form the delta, a vast area of wetland about twenty miles north of the Buenos Aires. The estuary is huge; and even at Buenos Aires, a hundred miles upstream, the Plate is over fifty miles wide. Later in the day the origins of its name became obvious, as in the rays of the setting sun it shimmered like an overlay of silver.

The mist was rapidly dispelled by the heat of the quickly-warming sun, and shortly after breakfast they steamed past the city of La Plata. Acclaimed for its university but more famous for the exploits of its football team, La Plata was also notable for its polluting abattoirs, causing it to swelter under a permanent layer of smoke-haze.

It was at about this juncture that Steve began feeling uneasy; not by anything to do with either his private life or the *Sombrero* - but by Whiskey, who obviously had no passport or visa. Okay, he never went ashore - well, not as far as either he or Michael were aware - preferring instead to remain in the vicinity of the galley. He had his litter tray - of sorts, a decrepit old roasting tin that wasn't fit for purpose but made a perfectly serviceable toilet. It was lined with torn strips of newspaper, a stack of which were maintained in the galley for whenever the fire needed lighting.

So, the animal had even become 'house trained'. The trouble was, rumour had it that while the *Sombrero* laid over in Buenos Aires their own little galley would be closed, both Steve and Michael transferring amidships to work turn about with the other lads. This was owing to the fact that in the absence of passengers and with many of the crew being ashore their galley would be surplus to requirements. Indeed, it seemed there'd be so little to do that Frederico Henrique was playing benefactor, decreeing that his staff would be split into 'watches', the First watch working one day, the Second the next, and so on. It was an arrangement that was almost unheard of. Fair enough, he could recall earlier in the year, when the freighter *Alice Springs* had spent weeks on the New Zealand coast. The men - or at least the catering staff - had been allowed to take the afternoons off so long as they agreed on a rota system, giving each a fair crack of the whip. But this was something different entirely; three, perhaps four whole days to do as one pleased in one of the world's greatest cities. And what was more, according to Frederico Henrique, their pay wouldn't be adversely affected. But the problem remained - what to do about Whisky?

'No worries,' assured Graham, a huge Australian deckhand who'd formed a trusting relationship with the feline, speaking to him whenever he passed, ruffling his fur; or more particularly, tickling his belly - one of Whisky's favourite treats. 'We'll look after him in the mess-room. He knows us all and he's adored by everyone. No, so long as you make certain he has plenty of grub, he'll be as right as ninepence.'

'So long as you're sure,' answered Steve, who felt as if a weight had been lifted. 'It'll be a great relief to us both, knowing he's being properly looked after. Thanks, Graham - and you can rely on us for his food.'

So, that was Whisky catered for; providing he didn't wander off, pussyfoot ashore and get lost or rounded up by the authorities. That was another thing, thought Steve, who up until then hadn't considered the likelihood of quarantine. He didn't even know if Argentina had any quarantine regulations; although he felt sure that it must given that the country's economy was almost entirely reliant on livestock. But regardless, it was something they would eventually have to consider because he knew very well that at home in the UK, quarantine was rigidly enforced; this was assuming, of course, that Whisky didn't go AWOL in the meantime.

With the Buenos Aires skyline now clear on the horizon the *Sombrero's* crew were abuzz, owing chiefly to the news that she'd be berthing at Puerto Nuevo. This was normal practice but welcome nevertheless, at least for the short term; for Puerto Nuevo was virtually in the heart of the city, just a stone's throw from the fabled Corrientes, Lavalle, Florida and all the other thoroughfares that made Buenos Aires so special. Less agreeable were the tidings that she'd eventually shift around to the Anglo, an abattoir and meat-packing plant in one of the less salubrious areas of the city. The abattoir was located alongside a putrid backwater in a barrio known as Dock Sud, a district south of La Boca and outside the BA city limits. All this was relayed by Michael who was positively glowing. 'And another thing,' he added, as he sank his opener into another can of Tuborg, 'it's the Nanny's birthday today, and she's invited the entire catering staff to a piss-up in a bar on Sarmiento. The bar owner doesn't know it yet but she's going up to see him this afternoon - and anyway, she reckons she'll need to unwind after being traumatised by a bunch of screaming kids.'

The stopover at Puerto Nuevo was purely to off-load the passengers, to spare them the ignominy of being dumped at the Anglo, as festering an outpost as you could imagine. According to most reports the *Sombrero* would be shifting in the morning. If this was true it'd be a blow to the crew as it would mean either a journey on the bus or a trip in a taxi to the night spots. That said, it wasn't a calamity for as Michael articulated, Dock Sud had its own attractions.

The sun was at its zenith by the time the *Sombrero* was secured. Her tugs had departed and a canvas-covered gangway was already in place as Steve joined Michael at the rail. As its name implied, Puerto Nuevo was a more modern part of the port which stretched along the Buenos Aires waterfront. They were berthed in Darsena Norte, the basin closest to the commercial district and one that was surprisingly tidy. Unlike many seaports where the wharves were cluttered Darsena Norte was featureless, save for the railway tracks leading to the marshalling yards. Beyond the railway the city lay waiting, a siren calling for her sailors - and her sailors wouldn't keep her waiting.

The *Sombrero* wasn't lacking in company for also occupying Darsena Norte were two modern freighters, each of them stylish and sleek. Sweden's Johnson Line who owned the *Rosario,* and the Hamburg, South-America Line, owners of the *Cap San Lorenzo,* were renowned for the excellence of their ship keeping - not a flake of rust and paintwork that dazzled in the sun.

Mail had arrived with the agent; postings from home that were repeatedly read before being carefully stowed away in wallets. Steve had received letters at Rio - one from his family, the other from his much-beloved grandmother. Now there were three letters more, including an epistle from Maxine who was apparently well but wishing that Steve was much closer. He reflected how badly he was missing her; although that hadn't prevented him from being disloyal when it suited. His thoughts drifted way back to Napier - back in April; and to Glenda, the part-Maori nurse with whom he'd romped like a rabbit as they sated their sexual voracity. Even after all this time he felt a sudden surge of guilt for being unfaithful to Maxine - but not so guilty that cheating couldn't feature in future.

And so, with the stove now redundant it was time to take stock of the galley, to rake out the coals and dispose of the still-glowing embers. Dinner had been simple and make-shift: Cornish pasties they'd had to reheat, with baked-beans or peas as a vegetable. This had been followed by semolina pudding and everyone had gone away happy. Many of the crew would have scampered ashore just as soon as they'd gobbled their dinners; but for Steve, cleaning out the fire was only one of the tasks on his 'to do' list.

With the smouldering ashes now outside in a bucket he doused them with a kettleful of water, causing them hiss and steam while drowning their propensity for harm. He could now dump them in the rosie with the rest of the rubbish to be safely disposed of later. Then there was the usual strapping up; not so much of it today, thankfully, and the utensils were soon neatly stowed. And then there was the need to empty the lockers and remove the provisions from the fridge. These he transported to the midships main galley where they'd doubtless disappear in the 'mix'. And finally, with the clean-down and scrub-out completed it was simply a matter of locking the doors and retiring - but not before Whisky was resettled.

Whisky was sleeping like a baby, in the shade of the awning that the deckies were soon to dismantle. Steve lifted him gently, placing him in his bed before carrying him down to the mess-room where Graham was waiting - along with a saucer of milk and a bowlful of fish and boiled chicken. Then, after fetching the litter tray and stroking his pal he departed to finish his chores, having remembered the still-to-be-emptied rosie. As an afterthought, as he left the mess-room he called over his shoulder that he'd be back again later with another consignment of chicken.

9

The bar on Sarmiento was the ideal venue for a party, the owner having gone to extraordinary lengths given the notice available to lay on decorations and food. And so it was that before eight o'clock the place was bouncing, mostly with those from the *Sombrero* although locals hadn't been thoughtlessly excluded. Indeed, almost the entire catering staff attended, with the exception of the Purser and Frederico Henrique who'd given it a miss and headed for the refinement of the Jockey Club. Another who was missing was the Laundryman; but he hadn't been expected and given that he was a misery his absence was viewed as a blessing. And as for the deckies and firemen, none of whom had been invited? Well, they'd probably headed for wherever, perhaps the Copper Kettle or the Texas Bar, both favourites with footloose British seamen. And then there were the few who were abstinent and were spending the evening at the Mission; or if there was a film to their liking, at one of the cinemas on Lavalle. Of one thing they could be absolutely sure, wherever they were they wouldn't be wanting for entertainment.

Rather surprisingly three officers were also in attendance; the Second and Third Mates and a deck cadet, a fellow on his first trip to sea. According to Jim the cadet was a stooge whom the mates were manipulating for amusement - and who by the end of the evening would be wishing he'd kept his own company.

One thing that didn't need explaining was the fact that the Third Mate was sweet on the Nanny, a beauty called Jenny who'd been let off the leash and was rapidly becoming paralytic. The officer was clearly displeased, watching her intently; hardly surprising given that for the past three weeks he'd been sharing her bed, and was known to be excessively jealous. Given this resentment the last thing he'd want was for the girl to get hopelessly sloshed, not caring who she jumped into the sack with.

Funnily enough, those who remained sober the longest were the contingent of five homosexuals, this despite their zest for gin and orange. Not so the hapless Second Steward, who after collapsing in a heap was bundled into a taxi which was despatched in the direction of the *Sombrero*.

And so, what about the lads from the galley? Well,Colin and Jim had disappeared, having gone for a stroll, ostensibly for a breath of fresh air although there was no telling where they eventually ended up. This left just Alan and Steve, the two youngest of the four, to manage using their own initiative. This they did with admirable conviction, even flagging down a taxi at around two in the morning having tumbled outside on the pavement. The taxi was an absolute must, as neither was capable of walking to the port - even if they'd known how to get there.

Steve watched befuddled as the taxi - a huge black Pontiac - roared away into the night as he swayed to and fro with the *Sombrero's* berth oddly empty. And then there was Alan, clutching his stomach and falling, writhing in agony with Steve an impotent spectator. And then there were the headlights; and a single-decker bus came rumbling towards them as if they were prospective passengers. As the bus drew to a halt the driver leapt out as the conductor flung open the doors. Alan was hoisted and tossed on to the floor while Steve was handcuffed to a handrail - and the rest was a cerebral void.

'Come on mate - time to get up. Christ, I've never seen anyone so smashed. It's a good job those coppers were decent and not like some of the arseholes.' Steve was being vigorously shaken, the speaker's words trying gamely to penetrate while he was unable to react. He was aware of a voice - somewhere in the ether, but it might as well have been on the moon. Then, by minuscule increments it gradually dawned that he was in his own bunk in the safety of his very own cabin. And then, the familiar face of the night-watchmen fuzzily drifted into focus. His head was exploding as he strove to recall how he came to be in bed when the last thing he remembered was being shackled to an omnibus' handrail.

Of course, it hadn't been a bus at all but the Argentine equivalent of a paddy-wagon, and both the driver and conductor had been policemen. A squinted glance out of the porthole revealed a grey slab of concrete and he knew immediately that they were no longer berthed at Puerto Nuevo. 'Where the hell are we?' he mumbled, propping himself up on an elbow while rubbing sleep from his eyes with his knuckles. 'We weren't here yesterday.'

'We shifted here during the night,' answered the watchman, 'while you were ashore. We're round at the Anglo - surrounded by shit and fuckin' blowflies? Fortunately for you those coppers discovered where the ship had been moved to and brought you back to the *Sombrero*.'

All sorts of clamour were resounding back and forth on the landward side of the porthole; the sounds of dockside machinery, voices either shouting or chattering away in Spanish - and that buzzing noise may have been blowflies. But the cacophony - whatever it was - was irrelevant, and seeing that Steve was in the land of the living the watchman departed, leaving Steve to get dressed and make his way down to the galley.

'Get back into bed you silly bugger,' groaned a voice from beneath him as Steve swung his legs over the bunk-board. 'You've got the day off. Alan and Colin drew the first watch and they've already turned to.'

The voice was Jim's, and he was reminding Steve that with the crew galley closed the watch system had begun and that he and Steve had drawn the 'Second Watch'. And then Steve remembered. The staff from the main galley, along with himself and Michael, had drawn lots to determine the watches, and he had been one of the more fortunate. Also not working were Michael, Derek, Lenny; and the assistant baker, a Scotsman from Oban who also liked a drink and who was at present sleeping it off in a police cell.

Steve was reawakened mid-morning, by the sounds echoing in through the porthole. He lay there, listening, trying to identify the noises, before at long last shifting his carcase. His mouth tasted vile and a drink was top of his agenda, tea or coffee being favourite - but first he ought to brush his teeth. But the extra hours' sleep had worked miracles and apart from his mouth he was feeling in pretty fine fettle. And as for Jim: he was perched on the settee, flicking through the pages of a newspaper. 'What've you got there?' asked Steve, as he climbed out of bed and into a clean pair of underpants.

'Local paper,' answered Jim, as he scanned the back page which carried a report of a soccer match. The match, a cup-tie, apparently, had been between teams called 'Vélez Sarsfield' and 'Newell's Old Boys' with the result being a two-all draw. 'Bloke delivered it twenty-minutes ago. It's handy to have around - tells you what's on at the pictures as well as all the news. There's even a report on a game between Arsenal and Spurs.'

Jim had now turned to the front page with Steve looking over his shoulder, digesting the boldly-printed headline. 'Cuba crisis easing', advised a journalist called Eduardo Aguilar, dealing with an item that had threatened world peace but which in both Washington and Moscow was belatedly demanding some sanity.

The paper was the Buenos Aires Herald, an English-speaking organ aimed principally at the ex-pat community along with

Anglicised visitors. It was also popular among other nationalities who were resident in the city and hoping to improve on the language. A prominent feature was an editorial in both Spanish and English - a valuable aid to translation.

Prior to the arrival of the Herald - which would be available daily - the only information from the outside world had been courtesy of the 'Sombrero Clarion'. This was a single-sheet newsletter produced by the Writer containing summaries of the news that he'd gleaned from the *Sombrero's* wireless office. But in the absence of passengers the Clarion had been temporarily suspended; but it was no big deal as the Herald said it all and was well worth the four Peso cover price.

'Fancy a mug of tea?' asked Steve, rising from the settee and slipping into T-shirt and trousers. 'I'm just going to freshen up - and you know what? I think I'll get myself some breakfast because believe it or not I'm beginning to feel a bit peckish.'

'Yeah - me too,' answered Jim, who'd turned to page five of the Herald and was struggling with the clues in the crossword. 'I could murder a hot bacon roll.'

Clutching two bacon rolls and a mug of tea, Steve was about to follow Jim from the galley when Alan shouted, 'Hey! Steve? Have you still got your money and cigarettes? Those fuckin' coppers pinched mine - and my new Ronson lighter.'

Steve sat his mug on a worktop and delved anxiously into his pockets, fearful that he too had been robbed. But no; Pesos, Rothman's and lighter were all where they should be. Relieved, he answered, 'No - everything's here. You sure they aren't in your pockets - or that you haven't stowed them in a drawer?'

'Absolutely sure,' declared Alan, who was showing no sign of a hangover - or the stomach cramps that had so painfully disabled him. 'I told you, it was them coppers - thieving bastards.'

Alan continued that he'd asked to see the Captain, to request another sub to replace the money that had been stolen. Steve looked askance, suddenly suspicious, wondering if his pal was being truthful. Was he, Steve wondered, trying to obtain an additional sub to supplement the one he was entitled to? This was virtually confirmed when Alan revealed that he wouldn't be mentioning the police, but would spin a yarn about how he'd been rolled and subsequently relieved of his possessions. Well, at least the tale sounded credible. Many a poor sailor had fallen victim to thugs when in no fit state to defend himself - and would doubtless do so in future. That said, it remained to be seen as to whether or not Alan was believed.

Alan's ruse was undoubtedly fuelled by the stinginess of Simpson Line subs. Currently it was three Pounds per person for boy ratings with seniors entitled to six. It initially sounded like a fortune, but when the rate of inflation was taken into account it didn't appear half so generous. Jim had already conveyed that three Pounds today would probably only purchase what two would have bought back in August. As usual, it appeared workmen's wages hadn't risen accordingly and there was talk of industrial unrest, although nothing had so far materialized.

In the event, Alan was believed and he came away from the Captain beaming, nine-hundred Pesos to the good. It was the equivalent of a three-Pound sub less what it was calculated he'd already spent. Of course, he was no better off in reality as the money was his own and would appear on his pay slip as a deduction.

'I'm slipping ashore for a livener,' announced Jim, glancing at his watch which now read midday precisely, 'fancy coming along - there are a couple of bars around the corner.'

'Yeah - why not,' answered Steve, who'd fully recovered from the effects of Jenny's party and was himself having trouble with the crossword, 'I'll have a go at finishing this later.'

And so he and Jim slipped ashore, becoming the butt of some banter from a gaggle of deckies who were busily touching up some paintwork - and to whom a day to yourself in Buenos Aires was the stuff of dreams in the real world.

'Envy'll get you nowhere,' mocked Jim, good naturedly, as he and Steve descended the gangway and on to the quayside where they immediately encountered a marinero.

'Buenas tardes, amigo,' greeted Jim, as he stepped around the uniformed figure, followed by Steve who smiled and was pleasantly acknowledged. The marinero, in this instance a youngster little more than a teenager, was in fact an Argentine naval rating who executed the security duties that in London would have been performed by a policeman. The difference was, that whereas the copper carried only a truncheon, the marinero was armed with a machine gun.

Dock Sud itself - after which the district was named - was an inlet off the Rio Riachuelo, itself a tributary of the Plate. The Riachuelo and the dock were septic, for in addition to the rubbish that polluted the water the surface was coated in oil. The oil was the product of a tank farm, further along from the Anglo and serviced by a procession of tankers. Owing to the frequency of their visits it seemed the tankers were working on the coast, transferring oil from the 'farm' to other locations along the estuary; perhaps to Necochea - or even as far as San Nicholas, way up the Paraná river.

The craft employed were diverse, ranging from relatively modern carriers to superannuated relics. Of the former; two carried the colours of Shell and were operated by that company's subsidiary, Estrella Maritima Argentina. These were the *Kellia* and the *Kalinga*,

93

both barely seven years old. At the other end of the spectrum one of the more venerable specimens was nudging a year over forty. She was the *Juncal,* a product of Armstrong-Whitworth's Tyneside yard in the years following the First World War. She had a vertical stem and a counter stern, all topped off with a Woodbine funnel. Now wholly owned by the Argentine company, Flota Argentina de Navigacion de Ultramar, her emergency steering position comprised an antiquated, wooden ship's wheel that was exposed to the elements, directly abaft the after deck house.

And so Steve and Jim ambled on, around the corner of the Anglo and on to a dusty road that headed in the direction of a bridge. But well before that they arrived at a concrete erection that squatted on an area of scrub-land. Above the doorway of the single-storey building ran a red and green neon-lit strip. It was nothing if not pretentious, and proclaimed this uninspiring hovel to be the world-renowned, ever-open, 'Welcome Bar'.

'We could have gone to the 'Nash,' offered Jim, nodding over the road at another shack, this one of wood and partially hidden in the grass. 'Trouble is, there are more flies in there than in this place.'

The Nash - or to use its full and much grander appellation, the 'Restaurant Internacional' - had a ripe reputation, not all of it wholly deserved. A drinking den and eating house of universal acclaim - so long as you didn't mind the flies - the Nash was remarkable for its enormous steak platters topped off with a giant fried egg. Indeed, it was said that if you'd eaten at the Nash then you wouldn't need feeding for a week, such was the generosity of its portions. And the price? Just twenty-five Pesos a plateful. But not only that that; you could drink yourself silly while ploughing through your meal for little more than double the cost.

But Steve and Jim were at the Welcome Bar - and what an ear-shattering welcome they received. Jim shoved open the doors and they were instantly deafened by a Perspex-topped Wurlitzer jukebox. The machine was living in a time-warp, belting out Paul Anka's 'Diana', years after it had peaked back in Britain. The immediate priority was to get as far from the jukebox as possible which was more easily considered than achieved. You see, the building was jammed to the rafters - owing to the arrival of the *Uruguay Star*.

The *Uruguay Star,* owned by the Blue Star Line of London so therefore by the Vesty family, was one of a class of ships already mentioned, and whose vocation it was to bring home the produce of the Pampas. She was a classic example of an integrated enterprise as the Vestys also owned the Anglo - or Frigorifico Anglo, to use its official title - the abattoir sitting on the dockside. As was plain from the *Sombrero's* presence the Anglo's produce wasn't shipped solely by its owners. It was also transported by other companies including Houlder Bros, Lamport & Holt, and Royal Mail.

The Vesty Corporation was huge, with worldwide interests in food production, most notably the farming of livestock. In fact, the organization was concerned with meat from the instant the animals were conceived until they arrived on the great British dinner plate. In addition to their Argentine ranches the Vestys owned facilities in Australia and New Zealand, the produce being shipped in the company's own fleet before being retailed in yet another family business, the Dewhurst chain of butcher's shops. That said, the most obvious sign of the company's operations were undoubtedly the 'Star' boats themselves.

So, this was it, first port of call for many a seaman on his first ever visit to Buenos Aires; and what a contrast, Steve thought, compared with the bar on Sarmiento. Of brown-panelled woodwork and crystal chandeliers there were none. Instead, the Welcome Bar catered for a more modest clientele; a clientele that was more likely to be dressed in dungarees or jeans rather than pretty frocks and suits. The furniture was time-worn and shabby, displaying the effects of spillages and cigarette burns that had created crazy patterns in the woodwork. Cigarette smoke hung in the air, the slowly-revolving ceiling fans stirring it up so that it drifted and mingled but never entirely dissipated. And then there were the flies, settling on everyone and everything having invaded the building from the slaughterhouse. If they were as bad as this in the Welcome Bar whatever must it be like in the Nash, thought Steve, swatting at a bluebottle that was either buzzing around his ears or threatening to drown in his lager.

They'd taken a table near the jukebox - the only one vacant for obvious reasons - where conversation was hopeless except in the intervals between records. Apart from themselves and a handful of others the crowd was from the *Uruguay Star*. There was a scattering of locals, probably dockworkers or others associated with the port, while women were conspicuously lacking. The latter was hardly surprising as regardless of its virtues the place was an unsavoury dump. But strangely, this insalubrious pigsty had the allure of a seductress and seldom, it seemed, could a seaman pass it by without being tempted through its doors. It was a form of fatal attraction, confirmed by Jim who related how on a previous occasion he'd popped in for a 'quickie' on his way up town and stumbled out well after midnight, supported by a couple of his shipmates.

But that wouldn't be happening on this occasion. 'Come on,' said Jim, after a couple of beers had sated their thirsts and the jukebox had pummelled their eardrums, 'let's go for a stroll. We'll walk as far as the bridge and then I'm going to get my head down - and if I were you I'd do likewise.'

They wandered in the direction of the river crossing, a Meccano-like colossus that could easily have been mistaken for a transporter bridge. In fact it was nothing of the sort. It was actually a road bridge that spanned the Rio Riachuelo, connecting the neighbourhood of La Boca with nearby Isla Macieo, a slum area south of the river. The structure was supported by tall concrete pillars that handily incorporated stairwells, enabling pedestrians to access the footways. The bridge was the 'Puente Nicolás Avellaneda'; and what gave it the appearance of a transporter-bridge was the massive steel over-span that hoisted the road allowing river traffic to pass underneath. Now over twenty years old, it was named after a former Argentine president.

However, if the Puente Nicolás Avellaneda wasn't a transporter-bridge then its neighbour most definitely was. A near fifty-year old veteran, the Puente Transpordador was the original crossing of the Riachuelo, and although now redundant there were no immediate plans for its disposal. Whatever, standing cheek by jowl only metres apart these architectural gems were phenomenal - which was more than could be said for their surroundings.

This was never truer than of a pool known as La Vuelta de Rocha, a gloomy lagoon a little upstream from the transporter bridge. Polluted and reeking it was a toxic dumping ground for obsolete and rotting river craft.

As for alternative river crossings: in addition to the bridge there was a ferry, a clinker-built craft that the ferryman rowed standing upright, facing the direction of passage. However, intending passengers had to be wary for although the boat was internally immaculate the exterior was coated with oil.

Indicating towards Isla Macieo, Jim pointed out a collection of sheet-metal dwellings that seamen referred to as 'Tin-Town'. Home to abattoir employees it was a ramshackle sprawl that was said to be a haven for bandits. Indeed, it was a frightful fact that throughout the hours of darkness taxi drivers refused to cross the bridge for fear of falling victim to ambush. In such situations the fares were dropped off in la Boca before completing their journeys on foot. And as for the seamen: they were advised to avoid Tin Town at all costs, especially at night when only the locals ventured out - and only then in the company of others.

But tonight's destination was greatly removed from the shanty-town. Rather, they'd take a bus from La Boca and make for the Flying Angel Mission before heading for Corrientes and a supper of either beefsteak or pizza. And so it was that at around eight o'clock the four 'compañeros' crossed the Rio Riachuelo and hopped on a brightly-coloured bus.

Yet, La Boca had a charm of its own, a colourful appeal that was well worth exploring although it was seldom ever mentioned in passing. You see, La Boca was the heart of the old sailor community, where sixty-years earlier immigrants had arrived in the hope of amassing their fortunes. Many had shipped out from Italy; but the British weren't lacking while neither were the Spanish or the French, not to mention Scandinavians and others. There were those who remained where they landed, including unattached seamen who in view of the rewards had decided to quit their vocation. They built their dwellings of sheet-iron and steel - from the adjacent shipyards, painting them in the most garish of colours, often with paint that they'd stolen. Unfortunately, this delightful corner of Buenos Aires, home to Tango and handicrafts, was routinely overlooked by the seamen of Steve's generation who, despite its attractions, regarded it as not worth a candle.

And so, the bus careered off; along the Avenida Almirante Brown towards Paseo Colon and the Plaza de Mayo, site of the Casa Rosada - the rose-coloured parliament building. Now then, Steve was no stranger to buses but Buenos Aires buses were legendary. Known affectionately as 'Colectivos', these vividly-coloured, single-deck vehicles hurtled through the streets as if in the Monte-Carlo Rally. Passengers had to be quick off the mark or they could either be left at the stop or carried past the stop they were wanting; and unless you boarded the bus at the beginning of the route it was typically standing-room only.

But it wasn't all a mad-hatter's tea-party, for although the colectivo wasn't the choicest form of transport it was ridiculously cheap, allowing the rider to travel for a pittance. Each colectivo line had its own allotted route with frequencies that in Britain were unheard of. The more heavily-used services operated at five-minute intervals, from soon after dawn until the early hours, with some running right through the night. The specimen that Steve and his pals had boarded was painted a startling yellow that incorporated the most intricate artwork. Like others on its route, it operated between La Boca and Estación Retiro, the principal rail terminus for train services north of Buenos Aires.

They left the bus on the Paseo Colon, at the junction with a dark and cobbled side street that gloried in the name of, Cochabamba. The journey couldn't have been easier as the streets of Buenos Aires follow the grid system and the colectivo, taking the direct route from La Boca to Retiro, had stopped right at the end of the side street. Steve was to discover that discounting right-angles, wherever you travelled in the capital the route was invariably linear; and if your eventual destination happened to lie along an intersecting thoroughfare then you never had too far to walk.

The Flying Angel - Mission to Seamen, was located only a short distance along Cochabamba, almost opposite a souvenir shop. The facilities available at the Mission were akin to those at most other Flying Angels - with the unexpected provision of a bar. Such a facility was virtually unheard in what was after all an associate of the Anglican church; but for whatever reason it existed in Buenos Aires and was cherished by the seamen it catered for. As regards stock: wines and spirits didn't feature, but there were beers aplenty and they only cost a handful of Pesos. 'Tell you what,' said Jim, strolling towards one of the snooker tables and depositing a coin in the light meter, 'we'll have a couple in here and then make our way to Corrientes. It's not very far and the walk'll help us work up an appetite.'

Steve never potted a ball, for try as he might he couldn't fathom the angles and invariably left a shot for his opponent. 'You're fuckin' useless,' complained Alan, his partner, as yet another red rebounded from a cushion allowing Colin to score an easy point. 'We'll be buying the beers at this rate.'

'Don't you blame me,' retorted Steve, glancing at the scoreboard which showed they were forty points adrift, 'you've only potted two reds yourself.' There was no denying that between them they were hopeless - at least where snooker was concerned, and a drubbing seemed a guaranteed cert.

However, their embarrassment was spared and their pockets secured by interruption from an unexpected quarter. Jim was lining up a shot which it seemed he couldn't miss when in walked four pretty maidens. This was totally unprecedented. Okay, you'd often find women at the Mission - helping to run the establishment, but not all dressed-up to the nines. But they were here; so cues were laid aside, introductions were made and acquaintanceships quickly cemented.

The girls, it transpired, were nurses from the 'Hospital Británico' - the British Hospital - and they'd called at the Mission to purposely socialize with seamen; British seamen, as it happened, although it soon became clear that friendship was a secondary objective. It rapidly emerged that their primary rationale was to improve on their mastery of the language, this despite the fact that their English was already superb. Whatever, friendships there were and they weren't to be casually scorned.

As you'd expect in a multi-racial community the girls had some fascinating names. First there was Helga - Helga Carrizo, whose mother was German and whose father was an Argentine tailor. She came from Rosario where her parents ran a clothiers assisted by her brothers and sisters. Marianela Evans was the daughter of a Chilean waitress and a hill-farmer from soggy mid-Wales, her family running sheep in faraway chilly Patagonia. Kari Lavezzi was a native of sunny Mendoza where her family produced wine, her Norwegian grandmother having married an Italian-born vintner. And finally there was Lara Kristensen, daughter of a Danish seaman and a Russian ballet dancer; although her father had fled at the first hint of pregnancy leaving her mother to cope single handed. Notwithstanding, it was a mosaic of ancestry; a classic indication of a harmonious cosmopolitan society.

There was certainly no lack of involvement. They discussed all manner of topics; the afore-mentioned family histories; the boys' lives at sea - tales that were often embellished but highly-amusing - why nursing was a chosen profession; how each of them was employed and what they aspired to in the future. Before the evening broke up Helga also impressed that this newly-established fellowship would be entirely platonic with transgressors being excluded from any further association. She went on to relate how a lad from Liverpool had once 'tried his luck' in the back of a taxi following an evening together at the cinema. Her eyes gleamed wickedly as she told how she'd grabbed him by the privates and almost tied them in a knot. The tale provoked laughter; but the lads were left in little doubt that the girl wasn't joking and meant precisely what she said.

But whatever the caveats it was proposed that they meet again tomorrow - perhaps go to the pictures before rounding off the evening with a meal. The girls were keen and it was agreed that they'd rendezvous at the Mission where they'd finalize venues and so on.

Immediately opposite the Mission stood Mary and Charlie's souvenir shop, an emporium of international acclaim. The place was a true Aladdin's Cave, with much of the stock being a spin-off of the cattle industry although the assortment of goods was mind-blowing. The girls had slipped off to wherever leaving the lads to their own devices - but not before they'd visited the souvenir shop.

Cow-hide handbags and wallets - belts, leather jackets and shoes; in fact, anything that could be reasonably produced from a bovine overcoat occupied niches and shelves. It was the variety of patterns that was most striking, in a medley of colours while smelling of freshly-cured leather, as if the skins had only recently been tanned. There was costume jewellery of all sorts: bracelets, necklaces and earrings - cufflinks, St Christophers and clasps; just some of the goodies that glistened under glass, alongside lockets and charms. The variety of watches was staggering, from vulgar-looking, mass-produced 'turnips' to those that were modestly expensive. Alan invested in a 'Zippo' - to replace his supposedly stolen Ronson - while Jim bought a brown leather waistcoat that was incredibly cheap and just too snazzy to resist. Steve, contrarily, bought nothing, preferring instead to hang on to his cash until he knew what he could afford.

And as for Mary and Charlie, the proprietors of the enterprise; Mary was dark-haired and tiny while Charlie was moustachioed and tall. They were not at all reticent, Charlie extending a hand towards Mary, with the greeting, in perfect English, 'Buenas Noches, Señors. This is my wife and I'm Charlie - welcome to our little venture.' Having doubtless Anglicised their names for the sake of the business it was a strategy that seemed to be working as indicated by the store's popularity. Whatever, they were both of middle-age and delightful, never pushy but willing to oblige.

102

Carrying on into the city they passed the pink-painted Casa Rosada where, it was said, bullet holes could still be seen in the walls, evidence of an earlier revolution. Although the seat of Argentine government and ostensibly a presidential mansion it didn't actually serve as a residence, the Head of State residing instead at Olivos, an affluent suburb to the north of the capital on the shores of the Rio de la Plata.

And so they arrived at the Avenida Corrientes, the most glamorous of thoroughfares; the heart of Buenos Aires theatre-land; home to Luna Park, a vast amusement and entertainment complex; and so many pizzerias and steakhouses that you could feast for a year and not enter the same eatery twice. Steve had quickly formed the opinion that Buenos Aires was a highly-energised metropolis, generally coming to life after ten o'clock at night and never really going back to sleep. The pavements were crammed, with revellers scurrying to wherever; between rotisserie and theatre or cinema and bar - or just lazily strolling through the streets. At this time of night most of the restaurants were packed; but you could purchase a pizza, eat it 'on the hoof' and no-one would give a second glance. There were the sounds of music and laughter; and of horns honking - taxi drivers urging unwary pedestrians to 'Get out of the way because believe it or not, I'll not be stopping for anyone'.

'Hang about - I'm just going to buy a box of matches,' called Jim, breaking away and heading for a glass-fronted cubicle that projected from the front of an otherwise anonymous office-block, 'shan't be a sec.'

The cubicle was in fact a kiosco, a retail outlet unique to the city of Buenos Aires. With access for the attendant via the building to which it was attached, a kiosco was a tiny bazaar that sold virtually everything a person might need, by day or by night; newspapers, cigarettes, matches, lighters and lighter-fuel, razor-blades, pens, confectionery, socks, stockings, chewing-gum, soap, toothpaste, shampoo, lipstick, batteries, aspirin, and so on - the list was infinite. Its presence announced by a neon-lit strip, a kiosco gave scarcely enough room for the incumbent, although from their seated position the stock could be easily accessed.

'I'm going to settle for a pizza,' announced Colin, after the four had searched vainly for a vacant table with the time on the run-up to midnight, 'otherwise we'll end up with nothing.'

'Suits us,' voiced Alan and Jim in unison, leaving Steve - who'd never even heard of pizza let alone eaten it - wondering exactly what the meal would consist of. But it wouldn't remain a mystery for long, that much was clear as they entered a bustling pizzeria.

'Now, what shall we have?' pondered Colin, staring at the mind-boggling alternatives, both in the window and under glass on the counter. After a few seconds deliberation, he declared, 'I think I'll have a slice topped with prawns - and maybe anchovies. What about you blokes?'

Alan and Jim scratched their heads, unable to make up their minds, while Steve hadn't a clue what was what. 'If you've never eaten pizza before then try something simple,' advised Colin, who could see that Steve was in awe and struggling with the selection on offer. 'Why not try cheese, ham, pineapple and pepperoni,' he suggested, pointing at an appetising roundel. 'That way you'll know what you're eating.'

'What's pepperoni?' asked Steve, to whom the ingredient was alien but sounded if it might be Italian.

'It's a cured and spiced beef sausage,' replied Colin, who was acting in an advisory capacity, not only for Steve but also for Alan and Jim. 'It's really tasty - and I'm a hundred per-cent certain you'll like it.'

Pizza could be bought by the slice, the quarter, the half or the whole while the prices were extremely affordable. In the end they settled for a quarter each of their eventual choices with Steve opting as Colin had advised. Steve's pizza was a savoury explosion. In fact, he'd never tasted anything like it and wished he'd invested in a half. They were flavours that were previously unheard of. Back in dreary old Britain he might have sampled either a ham or a cheese sandwich but never a sandwich made of both. But not only that: chunks of tinned pineapple were more usually associated with birthday parties; and as for pepperoni..................

Their 'puddings' were great cones of ice cream, purchased from an overworked street vendor. The flavours available were boundless, a contrast indeed to their customary strawberry or vanilla. Steve chose lemon and lime, a mouth-watering treat he felt sure he'd remember forever.

And so they carried on walking, licking their ice creams, the commotion of traffic growing louder by the second until they arrived at a junction - although this was no ordinary cross roads. This was the Plaza de la República where they were confronted by an almighty obelisk. The monument, which celebrated the city's foundation, stood in the centre of the plaza which itself formed the nucleus of the intersection. The intersecting thoroughfare was the Avenida 9 de Julio, the world's broadest artery, taking its name from the date of Argentina's independence. It was here that the revving of motors and the honking of horns was at its loudest, with eighteen lanes of traffic that were perpetually clogged with vehicles going nowhere in a hurry. The road was a pedestrian's nightmare, only safely navigated via a ladder of crossings and by obeying the myriad of traffic lights. You needed to have plenty of patience as depending upon the frequency and sequence of the signals this incredible highway could take between two and ten minutes to cross.

At one in the morning they sipped beer in a bar on Lavalle, the next street along from Corrientes. Lavalle was a paradise for film-goers, with any number of plush-looking cinemas which were a-dazzle with lights and where commissionaires greeted their patrons.

'Thinking about tomorrow, do you reckon we'll end up at the pictures?' queried Alan, stifling a yawn while nodding in the direction of the street.

'Tonight, you mean,' corrected Steve, glancing at his watch while walking around his stool in an effort to keep himself awake. 'It's already an hour past midnight.'

'You may depend we will,' assured Jim, answering Alan's query. 'It'll be a surprise to me if we don't.'

'So long as it isn't that soppy West Side Story,' rubbished Colin, not fancying a couple of hours purgatory when the likes of Billy Budd and Young Guns of Texas were also showing on Lavalle. 'The very thought of it makes me cringe.'

'So, West Side Story it is, then,' enthused Colin, rubbing his hands together and grinning, as if enjoying the prospect, 'and supper afterwards if we're lucky enough to find ourselves a table.' They were descending the steps from the Mission, *en route* to the bus-stop on nearby Paseo Colon.

'I've already booked one,' answered Helga, who seemed to be the girls' spokeswoman, and whom the others appeared to look up to. 'It's at a restaurant on Calle Esmeralda. The cuisine's excellent and it won't send us running to the bank.'

That was the one thing that Steve had been fearing; had he sufficient funds for both cinema and meals without going broke in the process? Whatever, it was too late to back-pedal now, but it was something to consider before making any further commitments.

Pedestrianized Lavalle was crowded, with film-goers heading for their venues and diners hunting for a meal - and the city hadn't yet come alive. As for the cinemas: in many respects they bore comparison with any in London although there were various and noteworthy contrasts. Whatever, they pushed through the throng until they arrived at their objective - and that was when Steve began fretting. In retrospect it was something he should have been aware of. Okay, there were posters galore and the film had been prominently publicised; but everything, it transpired, including the title, was boldly exhibited in Spanish. Oh! no, he thought, his spirits in jaw-dropping free-fall. How on earth can I sit through a couple of hours drivel without understanding the dialogue? We should have forgotten the girls and played snooker at the Mission instead. But, the die was cast; although that didn't prevent him voicing his very real misgivings.

'You needn't worry,' answered Lara, the semi-Nordic beauty with the flowing blonde hair who happened to be his partner for the evening, 'It's been retitled for the Spanish-speaking market. That's why it reads, *Amor Sin Barreras,* meaning, Love Without Barriers. The soundtrack will be in English but there'll be Spanish subtitles for the locals.'

'Phew! That's a relief,' answered Steve, now feeling a little less gloomy. 'No offence, but I was thinking about making a run for it.'

Lara tittered as she approached the box-office while Steve reached cautiously for his wallet. He peeled off a number of banknotes, counting out seventy Pesos before handing them to Lara who'd turned from the window and was excitingly clutching two tickets. On espying the money she waved it away, reproving, 'No, it's only thirty-five - we always pay for ourselves.'

And that was the pattern throughout; the girls always paid for themselves whether it be for meals, entertainment or both. That way, Steve supposed, they would never feel indebted to the boys - and it would discourage the latter from taking liberties. There was also the blessing that in the short term at least it would save Steve a great deal of money.

So, what of Argentine cinema etiquette? Well, all four girls enjoyed a cigarette but wouldn't dream of smoking in public, that kind of behaviour by virtuous young women being frowned upon in tasteful Buenos Aires. The boys, conversely, had been puffing merrily away from the instant they'd left the *Sombrero;* so, imagine their surprise on being told to extinguish their cigarettes as smoking in the cinema was prohibited. It wasn't what the lads had expected although Steve wasn't unduly perturbed. Indeed, he found it a pleasure to be able to appreciate a film without having to peer through a fog. Nor was there the annoying distraction of rustling popcorn, crisps being crunched or latecomers being shown to their seats. This was owing to no food being allowed in the auditorium, and the doors being closed from the moment the showing commenced.

And enjoy the performance he did, with West Side Story being nowhere near as leaden as he'd feared. Fair enough, it was primarily a film for the ladies but as musicals went it could have been a jolly sight worse. And as for the meal that Helga had booked at the restaurant on Calle Esmeralda; well, it was a typical Argentinian repast, with great hunks of beef overlapping the plates that themselves were as huge as dustbin lids.

So, another day to themselves but how should they best spend the time? Well, exploring was the logical answer, leaving the evenings free for the night-life. Disappointingly, the watch-keeping rota had effectively broken up the foursome - at least during the daytime - but it couldn't be helped and it was just an unfortunate frustration. It was a topic they discussed as they ploughed through their bacon and eggs. 'Fancy a trip out to Olivos?' asked Jim, at length, referring to the riverside suburb a twenty-minute journey from Retiro. 'It's really swanky - where all the upper-crust live and others you wouldn't believe.'

'Yeah - why not?' answered Steve, eventually, after swallowing a 'chewy' piece of streaky. 'You know best - I'm still a Johnny-come-lately.' Given this status as a newcomer he was happy to follow Jim's lead. In fact, he'd little or no alternative if he wanted to learn the geography as otherwise he'd probably go nowhere. But the day would come when he'd know about the outlying districts and everything these places had to offer - but that day wouldn't be today. As it happened Jim's suggestion sounded highly intriguing, the more so as it encompassed a train ride. So, Olivos it was; but before he went anywhere there was the matter of Whisky and his victuals

As he'd promised Graham, ensuring that Whisky had plenty to eat had become part of his morning routine, although he knew that the cat wouldn't starve. Indeed so happy and content did the moggy appear that it was a matter of contention as to whether - when the time arrived - he'd return to the galley or choose to remain with the deckhands. Still, what would be would be and didn't concern him at present. And so it was that with Derek in tow they set out for the station and Olivos.

Owing to the almost identical architecture they could easily have been back in Britain. In fact, they were standing on the concourse at Estación Retiro as the terminus echoed to announcements. The high arched roofs were uncannily reminiscent of those at Paddington and York, while in a parallel with London's Liverpool Street station some of the services were electrified. The 'electrics' were state-of-the-art and had been designed for the benefit of commuters - although what benefit they gained was arguable. Rather than in compartments they were seated in open saloons. The seats were in pairs, either side of a centre gangway with the seat-backs swinging on pivots. This enabled passengers - well, those fortunate enough to obtain a seat as overcrowding was generally chronic - to ride 'facing the engine' regardless of the direction of travel. The three from the *Sombrero* would be catching an electric although a seat was virtually assured, their journey being counter to the traffic flow.

Within twenty minutes of leaving Retiro they were standing on the esplanade at Olivos, surveying the mud-stained river as it slapped against the concrete balustrade. Oddly, it put Steve in mind of his summer holidays as a child, and of those years of early adolescence. He remembered the waves that had battered the shoreline at times of high tide and tempest; that first pint with his dad and that date with Jean from Waterlooville. Was that really half a lifetime ago? he thought, as he studied the silt-laden waters. Of course, it wasn't so very long at all - only a couple of years in fact since that most recent unforgettable holiday. Regardless, it certainly felt like half a lifetime, so much had happened in the interim.

However, it was only seventeen years - an entire lifetime from Steve's perspective - since the end of the Second World War, when conjecture had it that prominent Nazis had evaded the allies and scuttled off to Latin America. For instance, it was popularly supposed that following Germany's capitulation Hitler's lieutenant, Martin Bormann, had escaped to Argentina where, under an assumed name, he'd taken up residence in Olivos. But stories such as this were commonplace, how Nazi fugitives had sought post-war asylum in any country willing to tolerate them. Martin Bormann, it was rumoured, was only one of such, speculation suggesting that in addition to the property in Olivos he owned alternative retreats including a home in Ascuncion, the capital of neighbouring Paraguay. It was in Ascuncion that he reportedly fraternised with Dr Josef Mengele, the infamous Nazi death-camp physician whose very name had sparked dread among millions.

As they wandered the streets Steve found himself scrutinizing faces - of middle-aged men, wondering if they were refugee Nazis. But as the day wore on his mind turned to more present-day matters. It appeared that Bormann and his cronies were elsewhere, and all those he met on his visit to Olivos were well-to-do but innocent Argentines. And as for Martin Bormann: like the world at large Steve was to discover that it was never firmly established that he'd truly escaped to South America, more up-to-date theory suggesting that he had in fact never left Germany and had died on a street in Berlin. But whatever the truth of the matter Argentina did provide a temporary haven for the notorious Adolf Eichmann, the SS supremo who in 1960 was spirited from the country by Israeli agents and ultimately hanged for his war-crimes.

It was now mid-November, the Argentine spring, and the weather was comfortably warm. Temperatures hadn't yet reached the heights which, allied with BA's notorious humidity, made the summertime heat disagreeable. Nevertheless, there were other, non-meteorological factors at work, each having an impact on the climate. Steve had already noticed the dirty brown haze in the distance, hanging ominously over the city. This was evidence - if it was needed - of the pollution caused by vehicle exhaust and smoke from the abattoir chimneys. 'Christ! Just look at all that shite,' remarked Derek, who was also studying the sky while puffing away at a Woodbine. 'It certainly makes you think about the damage being done to our lungs.' He coughed - and stubbed out his Woodbine in an ashtray.

After walking and loafing - sitting and smoking and pausing for the occasional refreshment, they left the leafy suburb in the late afternoon and made their way back to Retiro. As the train wound its way through the suburbs Steve - an avid railway enthusiast since early childhood - wondered why so many of the wayside stations appeared so remarkably British. At the time it was something of an enigma; but he later discovered that British companies had invested heavily in the Argentine rail network, hence his familiarity with the infrastructure. Most of the remaining steam locomotives along with much of the rolling stock were also manifestly British, although by the 1960s American-built diesels were gradually displacing the 'steamers'. Another sign of the changing order were the electric trains that had carried them to and from Olivos, the work, he was told, of Japanese designers and craftsmen.

As the train made its approach to Retiro Derek announced that he'd be meeting Michael at the Texas Bar. 'See if I can keep him out of trouble,' said the cook, who'd taken a distinct liking to the Irishman in spite of his earlier reservations. 'Mind you, I must say that since that debacle in the Galleons he seems to have come to his senses.'

Hmmm! If only you knew, mused Steve, remembering Santander, where Michael had got sloshed, had misread the time and had ended up scalding his hands. But that apart, he had to admit that ever since then his mate had shown commendable restraint - although there'd been recent signs of a relapse.

They arrived at Retiro at the onset of the evening peak, to find the platforms awash with impatient home-going office workers. Like strap-hangers everywhere they hadn't a minute to live and there was the potential for serious injury. It soon became a fight for survival as Steve and his pals were swept from their seats by hordes of opportunist commuters. They poured into the train through the windows which had been left open to ventilate the coaches. The lads' salvation was their agility, as they fled along the corridor to the 'country' end where the platform was a little less crowded. Meanwhile, the less agile boarders were condemned to a journey in the gangway, with every seat taken before the train became stationary.

So, what about the boys as they escaped the mêlée and Derek took off to meet Michael? Well, they headed for the Catholic Mission where a dance was being held and where they'd arranged to meet Colin and Alan. But it was early yet so they took a roundabout route and embarked on a spell of window shopping. They strolled along the Calle Florida, home to the trendiest stores in Buenos Aires - and some of the costliest too. But even so, the prices - which were still extraordinarily reasonable by British standards - were an accurate reflection of the quality of the goods on offer, this being especially true of the shoe shops. Steve was attracted by some fine leather slip-ons at seven-hundred Pesos a pair - a paltry two quid or so in his own currency - although to have bought them would have drained his resources. He swore about the niggardly Simpson Line for not allowing a more generous sub; conveniently forgetting that if he'd been less profligate earlier in the trip - that guitar he'd bought back in Rio, for instance - he could doubtless have afforded the shoes.

And so, at around eight o'clock they arrived at the Roman Catholic Mission, a seafarers' sanctuary that wasn't shy of booze and where music and dancing were bywords. The place was jumping from the outset for the dance had begun and there was scarcely room to stick a pin. But the place couldn't thrive without customers; so having spotted their mates at the upstairs bar they shoved through the throng and made their way up to the balcony. Here, a mass of humanity was struggling to get served without any apparent success.

'It's fuckin' hopeless in here,' swore Colin, as he waved a Hundred-Peso note beneath the nose of a nun who seemed at the end of her tether, 'I've been standing here for twenty fuckin' minutes but no-one wants my fuckin' money.'

'Here - let me,' said Jim, nudging Colin aside while others complained that they'd been queueing for longer and that Jim should await his turn. 'Hey! Sister Teresa,' called Jim, ignoring the complainants while directing his shout at a habited figure who seemed less flustered than her harassed companions. There was no response so Jim called again and this time the figure responded, waving and calling his name.

'Señor Jim - so good to see you.' Sister Teresa made her way along the bar, squeezing past her aides while clutching a vodka and orange. She handed the glass to an oversized Swede who after paying his money, grunted and shuffled to a table. 'So - you're back again and you've brought your friends along with you. So nice to see you all - now, what can I get you to drink?'

Jim ordered four rum and cokes, grabbing the hundred Peso note that Colin had flourished so vainly. 'You keeping okay, Sister Teresa?' asked Jim, as the nun poured four tiny measures into half-pint tumblers then proceeded to drown it with coke. Colin and Alan glanced askance while Steve looked on in disbelief. For whatever reason, but probably owing to the fact that as members of a religious order they didn't know otherwise, the nuns leant heavily on the coke, believing that if the spirit was generously diluted there was less chance of their guests getting drunk.

'Yes, I'm keeping fine, thank you,' replied Sister Teresa in answer to the question. 'Busy, busy as usual,' she smiled, placing the glasses on the bar and taking the hundred-Peso note. 'As you can see,' she continued, diverting her attention to a Geordie lad who had been patiently waiting for ages, 'I can't talk now as there's so much to do - I'll try and catch up with you later.' That was a fact; there were only three of them serving when there really ought to have been six.

'You obviously know her, then,' commented Steve, as they pushed away from the bar and leant on the balcony rail, scanning the dancers below. Steve wasn't blind, and knew that beneath the habit was an extremely attractive young woman.

'Yeah - I've known her for over a year confirmed Jim,' taking a sip from his glass which may just as well have held lemonade. 'I met her on a bus the first time I came to BA. She was loaded with shopping and some of it had fallen on the floor. I helped pick it up and carry it back here and we've been pretty friendly ever since.'

'You'll be all right there, then,' chafed Alan, who was frowning at his glass, wondering what had happened to the spirit. 'It's not everyone gets the chance of a bit of rough and tumble with a skirt dressed up as a magpie.'

'Not on your life,' demurred Jim, throwing Alan a glance that hinted he was talking out of turn. She's a smashing bit of stuff I grant you, but I wouldn't try chancing my arm. I've got my self-respect - and respect for both her and those like her.'

That put Alan in his place although he still managed the final utterance. 'That's as maybe,' he remarked, a faraway look in his eyes, 'but that wouldn't stop me from trying.'

10

Upon waking the following morning it was obvious that something was amiss. Instead of the usual hubbub: shouted voices, the hum of machinery and all the other sounds associated with the waterfront, there was an abnormal hush, as if it was a Sunday or perhaps an unpublicised holiday. But Steve knew it wasn't a Sunday - and guessed a holiday was unlikely. He slumped back in his bunk, analysing the anomaly until curiosity prevailed and he stretched to look out of the porthole. And that's when the mystery deepened for instead of a marinero patrolling the quayside there was a platoon of heavily-armed soldiers. And that wasn't all: an armoured personnel-carrier was parked across the wharf barring anyone from entering or passing. By this time Colin was aroused, gazing at the scene on the quayside. 'What do you reckon that's all about?' asked Steve, as he climbed from his bunk and stepped into his dungarees.

'Haven't a clue,' replied Colin, who was stifling a yawn and displaying a distinct lack of interest, 'and what's fuckin' more I'm not bothered. It's my day off and I'm getting back into bed.'

'I'll just freshen up and then I'll go and ask Sec - see he knows anything,' volunteered Steve, as Colin snuggled under his blankets and drew the curtain to shut out the daylight. 'Something's clearly happened and it might put a stop to our shore leave.'

'That's a point,' answered Colin, who'd changed his tune in an instant, was suddenly alert and was already slipping out of his bunk. 'Hang about and I'll come with you.'

'The workers have all gone on strike,' answered the Second Steward, when Steve posed the question as to why everything was quiet at the slaughterhouse, 'and it's not just the abattoir either. It

116

seems like a general stoppage - the buses and trains aren't running and all the civic offices are closed.'

'How d'ya know that?' queried Colin, suspecting the tale was a leg-pull. 'The Agent told me,' replied Sec, sniffily, resenting the scepticism and miffed at being taken for an alarmist. 'They got him out of bed and gave him the news before daybreak. He drove straight here. He reckons there's troops everywhere and he had to show his pass at every checkpoint.'

'So, where does that leave us?' asked Steve, concerned that their shore leave would be cancelled. 'Does that mean we're confined to the *Sombrero*?'

'Agent didn't say so,' answered Sec, satisfied now that he was being believed and not being taken for a scare-monger. 'As far as I'm aware you can still go ashore - all the bars and cinemas will still be open, it's just that you'll either have to walk or take a taxi to reach them.'

'Well, that's something,' observed Steve, who'd been worried that they might become 'prisoners'. 'I don't mind walking, so long as we can still get ashore.'

'I s'pose it means we could become stranded,' enthused Colin, envisaging a prolonged layover in Buenos Aires stretching days - perhaps weeks into the future, 'at least until they call off the strike.'

'Not necessarily,' declared the Second Steward, glancing at his watch and edging ever further along the alleyway. 'Don't forget we've got a mail contract, so if the strike isn't over within a couple of days I can see us sailing as we are - that's assuming the tugs are still working, the pilots too, come to think of it.'

'So, what about the soldiers?' enquired Colin, 'what are they doing down on the quayside?'

'Extra security,' replied Sec, throwing the answer over his shoulder as he unlocked the door to the dry stores, 'to deter saboteurs. According to the Agent, they've already torched a factory in La Plata.'

So that was the story as it stood. It appeared that the Anglo's night-shift had walked out at midnight and the day-shift just hadn't clocked on. Strangely there was no sign of pickets, the sight of the soldiers doubtless a powerful deterrent. But all that apart; it was apparently a coordinated protest, organised by the unions, against the rising tide of inflation and the failure of wages to keep pace. It seemed that the bosses had dug in their heels and that in some instances strikers had gone on the rampage; and so there was deadlock, with no immediate prospect of a resolution.

'Well, at least we can still get ashore,' declared Steve, happier now that he knew that they wouldn't be constrained, 'although I don't know what we'll do when we get there.'

It was a question that was answered by the listings, courtesy of the Herald which was still in circulation after it had come to an agreement with its staff. 'I see that 'The Comancheros' is showing at a cinema out at Villa Lugano,' remarked Steve, as he studied the pages while sipping his mid-morning coffee. 'How far's that when it's at home.'

'Too far to walk,' replied Jim, who'd got to know the city like the back of his hand thanks to the frequent and comprehensive bus service. 'It's four miles at least - maybe five - way out in the south-western suburbs. If we went we'd have to take a cab.' And so, come seven that evening, after humming-and-hawing they finally headed for the outskirts, crossing the Rio Riachuelo and summoning a taxi in La Boca, with no hindrance whatsoever from the military.

If the up-market cinemas on Lavalle were classic examples of Art-Deco splendour, then the neighbourhood picture-house at Villa Lugano, with its almost entirely local clientele, was an insanitary, sordid little dump. Steve had even taken the trouble to tear the cinema listings from the Herald, for the taxi driver's guidance; now he was wishing that he hadn't. On a more positive note they had arrived early and were able to choose their own seats, avoiding those that were plastered with chewing-gum, but that apart it was virtually all down the 'Swanee'.

'What a fuckin' hole,' declared Alan, brushing crumbs from his seat that was to the right of the auditorium, roughly in the centre of the stalls. 'It's a pity you looked in the paper,' he continued, directing his comments at Steve who though ignoring the remark was thinking pretty much the same. 'Instead of coming here we could have spent the evening with the girls.'

But the decision had been made - they'd paid their money and the audience was swelling by the second. And what a rumbustious gathering it was, mostly young and exclusively male; hardly surprising given that generally speaking, westerns weren't the preference of ladies. There were whoops and cat-calls, there was verbal abuse, rubbish being hurled; while one of the yobs had even got a catapult protruding from his windcheater pocket.

'I can see there being trouble here,' murmured Jim, who'd been keeping an eye on two distinct groups who were responsible for most of the brouhaha. 'We'd better keep our wits about us - in case we have to leave in a hurry.'

It soon became clear that Jim had his finger on the pulse as the tribes separated, one towards the front, their adversaries several rows behind. Fortunately, both 'battalions' - for that's what they were as skirmishing was their common interest - were seated to the left, well away from the *Sombrero's* contingent.

'This is the Jets and the Sharks all over again,' whispered Colin, referring to West Side Story with its theme of American gang culture. But even so, the showing commenced and apart from the odd shouted insult the cinema was peaceful; so perhaps there wouldn't be a rough-house. And why should there be? They'd come to see The Comancheros - supposedly - which was highly entertaining, keeping the audience enthralled. Once again the sound track was in English with Spanish subtitles so at least they could understand the dialogue. And so, in the absence of any off-screen shenanigans the lads from the *Sombrero* were beginning to rest more easily; until, that is, it came to the sequence when the Indians laid siege to the ranch-house - and that's when the pot boiled over.

One of the louts, a member of the rearmost group, cleared his throat and spat a huge ball of phlegm in the direction of the enemy formation. The projectile had been unerringly aimed, missing everyone else until it splattered its intended target - the rowdiest hoodlum at the front. The loud-mouth went totally berserk. Wiping his neck with a scrap of rag that presumably passed for a handkerchief he turned and leapt over the stalls, followed *en masse* by his 'amigos'. There was no 'By your leave' to the other patrons who scrambled to get clear as combat ensued and the fleapit turned into a battlefield.

The lights came on; but the film remained running, an ineffectual aside as the projectionist became absorbed in the action.

Steve and his pals were astonished. They'd all seen punch-ups before, in Steve's case none more violent than a brawl at the Wharfie's Club in Brisbane; but this battle-royal at Villa Lugano was like something imported from the jungle. Bicycle chains appeared from nowhere as noses were smashed and eyebrows became hideously swollen. Steve felt certain he'd seen something glimmer - a blade, perhaps; and it looked very much as though another of the yobs was using a screwdriver as a rapier. One of the antagonists shrieked, leaping clear of the thrash, holding his cheek as blood spurted out through his fingers. He removed his hand from his face and an entire slice of flesh was left hanging, dangling by the skin until its owner shoved it back where it belonged. By this stage some of the seats had been dismembered - being utilized as weapons;

120

clubs for the most part although some of the more jagged pieces seemed purpose-made for gouging out eyes.

Although those not involved in the engagement had fled the immediate battleground they hadn't in fact left the theatre, choosing instead to remain as mesmerized onlookers. These included Steve and his pals who were utterly speechless and couldn't believe what they were seeing. They stood at the rear, morbidly fascinated as the management, initially inert, eventually regrouped and set about restoring some order. This they achieved by setting loose three large Alsatians who tore into the fray, snarling and snapping at random. The dogs had been diligently trained as they weren't the least bit interested in the bystanders, only in those causing mayhem. One of the animals, a particularly vicious piece of work who was clearly a canine sadist, ripped the seat from the jeans of one belligerent who ran screaming from the house, clutching his buttocks that appeared to have been put through a shredder.

The dogs were having a field day; but had their amusement curtailed as they were recalled by their masters, the wailing of sirens announcing the arrival of police. As an additional measure the constabulary was supported by the army, a precaution should the disturbance be in anyway related to the current industrial unrest. By this time the cinema was emptying as the crowd evaporated, leaving only the wounded to receive a supplementary beating at the hands of the troops and police. Completely helpless, Steve merely winced as one of the soldiers, a scar-faced degenerate with obvious medieval tendencies, used the butt of his rifle as a battering-ram, shattering a teenager's teeth after the youngster had unwisely given lip. 'Come on - let's get out of here,' called Jim, from further down the street as the others lagged behind, glued to the ongoing drama, 'before they get the idea that we might be somehow involved.'

They didn't run, trying to stay out of the spotlight, walking instead at a lively pace until the war-zone was some way behind them. It was only then that they hailed a taxi - to the Flying Angel where they could meet with the girls and hopefully recover their senses.

It was destined to be one of those evenings; and it didn't improve as sometime around midnight they arrived at La Boca as they made their way back to the *Sombrero*. As they very well knew the taxi wouldn't cross the Riachuelo, the driver dropping his fare on what was generally considered the less 'hostile' shore of the tributary. And so it was as they drew to a halt that the 'cabby' demanded his fare. They each fished about in their pockets, gathering together a bundle of Pesos that in the cab's dim interior was virtually impossible to count.

As they alighted the taxi the area was magically deserted - fortunately so, for as Colin handed the driver his banknotes, he shouted, 'Okay, you three - leg it!' So, they all shot off, over the bridge without pausing to question the urgency.

'Phew! I'm not as fit as I ought to be?' announced Steve, eventually, as he squatted on his haunches while recovering his breath, the four having gained the furthest reaches of the Puente Nicolás Avellaneda. 'Anyway, what was that all about? We hadn't done anything so why the hundred-metres dash?'

'To get as far away as possible,' panted Colin, grinning cunningly as he brushed sweat from his brow and threw a glance in the direction of La Boca where the cabby was still counting out his cash. 'The fare came to four-hundred Pesos - but that bundle was two-hundred short so that's why we had to get a shift on. Anyway, I thought, by the time he finds out he's been diddled we'll be aboard the *Sombrero*.'

But Jim wasn't overly impressed. 'You bloody idiot,' he admonished, shaking his head as if Colin was a fully-fledged numbskull, 'You realize you've dropped us in the shit?'

How?' demanded Colin, who'd thought it'd be clever to swindle the driver while saving themselves two-hundred Pesos. 'He won't dare cross the bridge so I can't see why you're making such a fuss.'

'I know he won't cross the bridge,' answered Jim, who was way ahead of Colin in terms of cerebral alacrity, 'but he'll be able to recognize us. He'll call the cops - and they're not idiots. They'll know that we're seamen, from either the *Uruguay Star* or the *Sombrero* - and if we're not back on board then we'll be in either the Nash or the Welcome Bar.'

'And that's not forgetting the soldiers,' contributed Alan, remembering the brutality at Villa Lugano. 'I don't want to get on the wrong side of them bastards.'

'Me neither,' added Steve, forming a vivid picture of the youth having his teeth smashed with a rifle butt. 'They're nothing but a bunch of fuckin' thugs.'

'Hmmm........I hadn't thought of that,' ceded Colin, sheepishly, as he belatedly pondered his rashness. 'So, what do we do now, then?'

'Well, as far as I can see there's only one thing we can do,' rejoined Jim, nodding over his shoulder as he racked his brains for a solution. 'We'll have to carry on into Tin-Town - they won't think of looking for us there.' And so they resumed walking, down into Isla Macieo where there was no telling what lurked in the shadows.

And shadows there were in abundance, the only gleams of light escaping from shutter-clad windows - until they rounded a corner and were confronted by a bar called 'El Gato'. Here there was light in profusion, the name of the bar in a green neon strip with another in the form of a cat.

'What d'ya reckon?' asked Jim, peering up and down the street and then again at the door of El Gato, not entirely sure of his intentions, 'shall we chance it?' There was the lilting and haunting sound of music - Tango most likely, enticing them inside, followed by a round of applause.

'Come on, let's give it a go,' said Colin, eventually, making the decision for them all. 'It's just a little local cantina so I can't see them causing any grief.'

Steve wasn't totally convinced, remembering Jim's words when the *Sombrero* had moved round to the Anglo; how strangers weren't welcome in Tin-Town, and how they'd be foolish to go there after dark. But he followed his companions regardless, the tail-end Charlie as they stepped over the threshold and entered the bar called El Gato.

It was as if someone had switched off the wireless. No sooner had the boys made their entrance then the musicians: a guitarist, a pianist and a violinist, fell silent; the dancers became rooted while those at the tables who up until then had been happily conversing, lapsed into an uneasy quiet. The hush was deafening, the only utterance being a guttural growl from yet another Alsatian, its leash thankfully tied to a door-knob. Every eye in the building was now focussed on the four from the *Sombrero*, four silly sods who'd encroached where they weren't really wanted. It was a fearful stand-off - a matter of who'd blink first. The night was warm; but Steve still shivered, a bead of perspiration trickling down his back and beneath the waistband of his trousers.

The ice was broken by the barman; in the most unprecedented fashion - totally unexpected in a place like the bar called El Gato. His English was excellently spoken, delivered with a west-country burr. 'What will it be, lads? Four rum and cokes or four of our locally-brewed beers?'

Steve couldn't hide his amazement; a friendly-sounding voice when the least he'd expected was to have been dumped in the street on his backside. All four breathed a sigh of relief, laughing nervously as they drank in the scene and witnessed the lessening of hostility. Okay, each was still wary of the other; but the frost had been eased and there were tangible signs of a thaw.

It was Jim who responded, addressing the barman - but not on the issue of beverages. 'Where on earth do you come from?' he asked, hardly able to believe that he was speaking to an Englishman in the bowels of an Argentine slum.

'Bristol - originally,' answered their ruddy-faced saviour who was built like an ox and was reaching for a bottle of Bacardi, 'but not for the past thirty years. I jumped a Houlder Line boat after meeting a waitress in the Nash. It was love at first sight and we were married before the ship sailed. We've never looked back. That's her - over there,' he continued, nodding fondly towards a stunning señora of graceful middle-age who was dancing with one of the patrons. We've lived here happily ever since - got three grown-up boys and they all work over at the Anglo, although they're all on strike at the moment. Now then, what's it to be? Will it be the beers or will it be the four rum and cokes?'

They settled for the beers, their mouths being dry, most likely from nervous exhaustion. But all things considered their eventual acceptance was illuminating, especially given what they'd been led to believe of the creatures from Isla Maceio. Rather, it was abundantly clear that they were simply run-of-the-mill Argentines, now happily relaxed and at ease with the lads from the *Sombrero*. Upon reflection - and in light of his own apprehension - it appeared that if anything, these very same folk had felt more highly intimidated by the boys rather than the anticipated opposite. Thankfully, from whichever perspective, any real threat had dissipated - courtesy of a 'diplomat' from Bristol.

And as for the bar called El Gato: well, It's steel-sheathed façade and dingy surroundings did little to vindicate its innards. It was spotlessly clean, comfortably furnished; and it was clear to one and all that Dick Langley, the erstwhile Bristolian proprietor, barman - and as it turned out, Head Brewer - would sanction no unruly behaviour.

'Here, let me show you this,' he invited, beckoning the boys to the rear of the bar, past a small but scrupulously-clean living quarters. They eventually arrived at an outhouse where several large vats and a tangle of pipework gave the impression of a back-street distillery. 'There, what do you think of that?' he asked, as proud as a peacock, as if showing off some magical invention that not even Archimedes would have dreamt of.

'What the hell is it?' asked Alan, staring at Dick, as baffled as his three companions. 'Looks like some kind of chemistry set - only a hundred times bigger.'

'Well, I suppose it is - in a way,' answered their host, beaming like a crazy professor who'd just stumbled on a unique discovery. 'But actually it's my own little brewery, where I brew the very beer that you're drinking.'

Steve was still carrying his beer; a frothy concoction that tasted like nothing on earth - both bitter and sweet with an earthiness that defied definition. It was as black as the night with a pungency that would have stifled a skunk. 'What's it made of?' he asked, taking just a tiny sip as to have guzzled it would have made him throw up.

'Well, malt and hops, obviously - but onions, mostly,' answered Dick, enthusiastically, as if the product had all the hallmarks of Guinness but without the international acclaim, 'along with garlic and yeast - sugar, of course, and a few other ingredients that I vary to keep the clients happy.'

'And does it keep them happy?' prompted Jim, wondering what kind of people would consume this tipple unless there was no alternative.

'You can bet your life it does,' affirmed Dick, who clearly wasn't brewing it for his health. 'For a start, it's only a quarter of the price of traditional beers and for another, it serves as a cleanser.'

'How come?' demanded Steve, who failed to see any correlation between this preposterous ale and say, a tablet of carbolic soap; although he had to concede that it would probably strip varnish from wood. 'From what you say it doesn't contain soda or detergent.'

'No, of course it doesn't,' agreed the Head Brewer of the bar called El Gato, 'and I have to admit that it does have an acquired taste. But you have to remember that the majority of my customers work in the slaughterhouse and that place is fuckin' disgusting. Just you imagine working an entire eight hours in that kind of environment. There's the constant whiff of blood, of steaming animal guts not to mention all sorts of unspeakable and slimy body fluids - you know, excrement, urine and snot. The incredible stench from that kind of stuff just hangs in your throat and nostrils, for hours after you've finished your shift and is enough to put you off your food. So, my onion beer is the perfect antidote. I tell you, a couple of glasses of that and you'll soon have an appetite for dinner.'

Steve was left reflecting which was worse, the beer or toiling in the slaughterhouse. He decided that all things considered he'd unquestionably opt for the former.

But Dick hadn't finished his tale; and he continued at length about conditions in the abattoir at large, before concluding, 'And the worst I ever heard was of a truck that arrived from the pampas with thirty-head of cattle for slaughter. One of the beasts had fallen, with its legs protruding through the slats. It meant the truck couldn't pass through the abattoir gates and was holding up the traffic behind. So, instead of wasting valuable production time in trying to lift the animal, some cruel bastard just chopped off its legs with a cleaver.'

Steve shuddered - and it wasn't just the sickliness of the beer. Dick's graphic account of slaughterhouse procedure had now focussed his attention on beef, and of how the meat ended up on his dinner plate. He found it harrowing; and he wasn't even sure if he'd ever eat beefsteak again.

'I've heard similar stories,' declared Jim, as they returned to the bar while Dick closed the door to his brewery, 'you know, how poorly the Argentines treat animals. But,' he added, as he emptied the remains of his onion beer into the soil surrounding a pot plant, 'it doesn't stretch to horses and dogs - they worship them as if they were gods.'

'That's right,' agreed Dick, who having locked up his brewery had caught up with the lads and was gathering up lagers from a shelf. 'But beef is the mainstay of the Argentine economy so the cattle are simply a commodity - no different from iron-ore or coal. But I agree, there's no excuse for ill-treatment - although some of our convicts, especially the political prisoners, are no better treated than the cattle. Here, have these on me,' he smiled, placing four foaming lagers on the bar, 'it'll make us quits after I foisted you those awful onion beers. Mind you.' he added, pointedly, eyeing-up Jim with just a hint of mischief, 'if that azalea dies I'll expect to be handsomely compensated.'

It was three in the morning when they vacated the bar called El Gato, the last of the customers to leave. Dick stood in the doorway, clutching a scarred table leg that was most commonly used in dealing with hooligans and thieves. 'Just be careful,' he warned, scanning the shadows where anything or nothing might be hiding. 'You should be safe, especially the four of you together - but there's no telling with some of these bastards. They more often than not work in gangs.' He kept watch until the lads disappeared, enveloped in darkness, should any of those for which the area was notorious view them as an easy source of income.

But the lads were acutely alert, glancing over their shoulders and into each darkened alley should rogues be planning an assault. In fact, Colin carried a nifty deterrent - a Swiss-army penknife that nestled in his left trouser pocket. As yet, it had only seen service as a can-opener, or for the trimming of his fingernails and toenails - but it could prove vital for self-preservation.

'So, what did you think of El Gato?' asked Steve, as they emerged from the gloom and into the relative brightness at the approach to the Puente Nicolás Avellaneda. 'I thought it was bloody fantastic - although for a while I was shaking like a leaf.'

'You weren't the only one,' added Alan, who'd felt like Jew in a mosque and had feared for his life at the outset. 'I was shitting myself until Dick turned out to be English.'

'But what about that brewery?' intervened Colin, changing the subject for no other reason than his fixation with alcohol of all sorts. 'It must have taken ages to build - you know, get all the bits and pieces together, assemble it and make sure that it worked.'

'Absolutely,' agreed Steve, remembering the outhouse that was more like a laboratory than a brewery. 'It's just a shame about that lousy onion beer. But there again, he obviously knew what he was a up to. After a couple of those you'd be ready for three or four Carling.'

'And what about that missus of his?' resumed Alan, who was sexually obsessed although as far as anyone knew he hadn't got his end away this trip. 'Ursula, that was her name, wasn't it? Cor! What a cracker - and she must have been the best part of fifty. Phwaaar........I could give her one any day and no mistake.'

'Good job Dick can't hear you,' chided Jim, who'd decided Alan's chatter was just superficial bluster to conceal his ongoing jitters, 'or he'd whack you around the ears with that table leg.'

By now they were on the dusty road that led to the Nash and the Welcome Bar and ultimately back to the *Sombrero*. But there were still shadows galore while the bushes and scrub were ideal hiding places for robbers. However, there were troops in the distance; and although they'd seen enough of the Argentine army to know that it wasn't to be messed with they'd feel happier surrounded by soldiers. So, all things considered - discounting the earlier aberrations - it appeared their evening would draw to a calm and untroubled conclusion.

But in fact it got a bloody sight worse, long before they reached the questionable safety of the soldiers.

Hey! What was that?' barked Alan, jumping in alarm and pointing at a patch of scrub immediately to the side of the Welcome Bar.

'What was what?' answered Jim, who like Colin and Steve had heard nothing, and guessed that Alan was suffering another attack of the collywobbles. 'There's nothing there - you can see that from here. It was probably just the wind in the leaves.'

Alan was gripping Steve's arm. 'Oh no it wasn't,' he answered, sticking to his guns like a limpet clinging to a breakwater. 'There's something or someone in there I tell you. There - there it is again........hear it?'

And this time the others heard it too. Yes, there was certainly a rustling noise - and there was also some grunting and snuffling. So, what to do now: did they investigate or did they walk on and ignore it? Fortunately, some of the light from the Anglo played along this stretch of road so it wasn't quite as dark as it might have been. As was his wont it was Jim who was initially motivated, venturing into the scrub, the others following some way behind. And it wasn't long before they discovered the source of the noises for there, half-hidden in the grass and incapably drunk lay Derek and Michael, blissfully asleep and snorting like pigs in a farmyard.

'Christ! Just look at the state of that,' exclaimed Jim, nudging Michael's leg with the toe of his shoe, eliciting an 'oink' for his trouble. He stood scratching his head, wondering at the best course of action. After a period of deliberation, he announced, 'Well, we can't just leave them here to sleep it off - we'll somehow have to take them with us.'

'And how do you propose we do that?' demanded Colin, who was slapping Derek's face, hoping to induce some awareness. 'They're too bloody heavy to lift.'

'I suppose we could try and find a wheelbarrow,' proposed Alan, limply, for want of a better suggestion.

'Don't be so bloody daft,' rebuffed Jim, who was doing his best to find a practical solution to the problem, and to whom silly suggestions were a distraction, 'where are we going to find a wheelbarrow around here at this time of night?' Alan shrugged his shoulders and fell silent, more than content to let the others do the thinking.

'Come on,' said Steve, at length, after manoeuvring Michael semi-vertical, although the cook was still snorting like a boar, 'heavy or not, surely we can carry them between us.'

And that's how they eventually proceeded, by slinging a lifeless arm around each of their shoulders and hauling the derelicts upright. But progress was painfully slow. 'Jeeez! This'll take ages,' complained Colin, as he and Alan dragged Derek through the dust, the leather being scuffed from his brogues.

Steve and Jim were equally encumbered although Michael was a shade more cooperative, managing four or five steps before he buckled at the knees and the boys had to make readjustments. Fortunately, a chain-link fence provided respite, where they could prop their burdens while panting and gathering their senses. They eventually resumed; until finally - and not a minute too soon as they were totally exhausted - they arrived on the quay where a posse of soldiers was waiting to scrutinize their papers. Wisely they were carrying their documents........but were Derek and Michael doing likewise?

Thankfully they were, for after delving around in various pockets the lads found the necessary paperwork, crumpled but wholly intact. After perusing the ID cards and visas the soldiers declared themselves satisfied, handing them back while laughing at the two drunken seamen. 'Mucho cerveza,' laughed the more senior of the men who was probably a non-commissioned officer although the boys didn't recognize his insignia.

'Si, si - demesiado cerveza,' trilled Jim, employing his Sunday-best Spanish, good-humouring the troops while eyeing the adjacent *Sombrero.* 'Mucho esfuerzo,' he added, trying to convey that it would take a great deal of effort to manhandle the cooks up the gangway. The soldiers clearly understood, ushering the lads past with Derek and Michael draped between them. It was nearly over, and another ten minutes should see them safely in their cabins.

But that wasn't the end of it by any means, for concealed in the shadows while all this was going on was someone who hadn't been so thoughtful. The sailors' peggy was in a flap, ruing the fact that he'd forgotten his Argentine visa. He hadn't a clue what to do to get out of this fix so he did the first thing that entered his head - he made a madcap dash for the gangway.

The look on Steve's face said it all; complete amazement as the figure zipped past, steaming like cross-channel ferry. At the very same instant came a cry, 'Alto! Alto!' as the soldiers, caught on the hop, demanded that the silhouette stop. But the terrified peggy ignored them, racing instead for the *Sombrero.*

'Here - quick, get down,' shouted Jim, dropping Michael in a heap as the others made a dive for the concrete. They lay flat on the ground, tensed-up and hushed as the drama gathered pace, rapidly approached its climax. No-one knew for sure what would happen -

but when it did they were totally mortified. Surely not, thought Steve, as another soldier, slightly further away and suspecting a would-be saboteur, unslung his rifle and shakily took aim at the fugitive.

The trooper faltered, suggesting he was a rookie - most likely a teenage conscript; but that brief hesitation proved priceless. By this time the peggy had been recognised and Steve yelled for him to give himself up; better to be arrested, he thought, than to be shot for the want of a visa. But the peggy was well passed reasoning and continued his sprint - then something extraordinary happened.

The finger was tightening on the trigger when another shape, this one much smaller than the first, dashed between a wobbly pair of legs, throwing their owner off balance. The shot resounded in the night, echoing back and forth between the walls of the Anglo and the vessels tied-up along the quay. The sound of the ricocheting bullet, whining and clanging - clattering and banging, was as frightening as the rifle shot itself. But that brief interlude, when everyone on the quayside and anyone else who'd been watching was temporarily rooted to the spot, had allowed sufficient time for the peggy to make good his escape.

'Whisky,' breathed Steve, sweating and shaking but grinning from earlobe to earlobe. He'd never been previously persuaded; but he now knew for certain that the cat did go ashore and for that he'd be eternally grateful.

They arose circumspectly - with the exception of Derek and Michael who were still sleeping the sleep of the graveyard - dusting themselves down as soldiers hurried past and surrounded their trigger-happy colleague. It became immediately clear that the fellow was the subject of a bollocking, receiving a particular earful from the guy with the insignia who plainly wasn't happy with the youngster. It appeared that in his mind at least, arresting the suspect would have been preferable to blasting his head off.

But happily the peggy had survived - head still intact - and on boarding the *Sombrero* had made straight for the mess-room where he hoped to find safety in numbers. The lads, meanwhile - assisted by Graham who just happened to be the gangway watchman and had observed the unfolding drama - were manoeuvring the cooks into the sanctuary of their shared accommodation, rolling Michael into his bunk while Derek was dumped on the sofa. 'His is the top bunk,' explained Colin, as he covered him with a blanket before easing the door shut behind him, 'and I'm not getting a rupture on his account. He'll be okay - although he'll feel like crap in the morning.'

And so to check up on the peggy, not to mention Whisky who'd vanished in a blur and might be anywhere by this time. As his mates drifted back to their cabin, animatedly discussing the various aspects of what had indisputably been a memorable evening, Steve followed Graham, across the after well-deck and into the mess-room where the peggy sat trembling like an aspen. 'You silly bugger,' rebuked Graham, although not unkindly as the poor little sod was still clearly upset and in a state of mind-numbing shock. 'Why didn't you just explain that you'd forgotten your papers? They would have come to some arrangement - maybe sent someone aboard to check that you were really who you said you were.'

By this time the lad was in tears. 'I can't speak Spanish,' he sobbed, as he dabbed at his eyes with a pantry cloth that Steve had found lying by the sink. 'And anyway - I thought I was in for a hiding whatever so I suppose I just panicked and ran. I guess they'll come looking for me now?'

'You can bet your life they'll be making enquiries,' agreed Graham, who had his head screwed on and wasn't going to make rash promises. 'So if I were you I'd get straight off to bed and stay there until you hear otherwise. I'll have a word with the Bosun, explain what's happened and see if we can't smooth it over -

although he's not going to thank me for giving him a shake at this hour.'

While Graham was playing Advocate General Steve went to check up on Whisky; and there he lay, fast asleep in his bed as if butter wouldn't melt in his mouth. Over the following weeks the moggy would be generously fêted, especially by the peggy who knew very well that he owed his existence to the cat.

In the event they needn't have worried. The army didn't come looking which was a relief and a surprise to everyone - not least the peggy who lay quivering in his bunk while awaiting that knock at the door. It was supposed that the incident - which had largely arisen owing to a squad-member's funk - had been sidelined, the troops overlooking the matter as a cover-up to protect their comrade. Leastways, this was how Steve was viewing it as he lay in his bunk, mulling over what by any stretch of the imagination had been petrifying. He couldn't sleep - how could he, with all this whirring round in his noddle? People firing guns at other people? Surely, that was the world of the Mafia, not ordinary folk: and certainly not the peggy who'd made a mistake but was definitely no saboteur. Still, at least he had the day to himself so he could gather his wits and assess the situation as it stood. And this resulted in the most uncanny conclusion of them all. No one, it seemed, apart from those directly involved along with Graham the gangway watchman, seemed remotely aware of what in any other sphere would have been headline news in the papers.

11

So, what should he do with day to himself but no-one to share his free time with. Jim was still asleep, the others were working leaving Steve with a distinct lack of fellowship; and that was his overriding demon. As already related he hadn't slept for twenty-four hours and his mind was in a whirl, unable to forget what might have been a fatal encounter. He needed some form of distraction but he couldn't think of anything apt. Sightseeing? Exploring? No! He'd already thought about both; and anyway, he couldn't even concentrate on the crossword let alone play the studious tourist. So, how to spend what he fervently hoped would be a less stressful day than its predecessor?

But then something went 'pop' in his head and he instantly brightened. What with the ferment of the intervening hours he'd completely forgotten that later that evening he had a date with the delectable Lara. They'd made the arrangement at the Mission, following the battle of Villa Lugano. Steve had been pleasantly surprised, her enthusiasm being totally unexpected when he'd suggested they go for a stroll, perhaps for a drink before rounding off the evening with a meal. He'd been anticipating refusal, wrongly assuming the girls never went anywhere unless Helga was present as chaperone. Now he had something to look forward to - but how to fill the hours in the meantime?

Well, for a start he ambled down to the galley, nicked a roll from the bakery and after cramming it with cheese, poured himself a mug of strong coffee. So, with breakfast made ready he strolled out on deck, cheese roll in one hand, coffee in the other and stood gazing at the scene on the quayside. In fact, it appeared very much as it had; a cordon of soldiers was strung along the wharf while the Anglo stood eerily still.

He was standing forward of the superstructure, adjacent to the screened-off swimming pool, immediately abaft number three hatch. Normally, this area would have been buzzing, with chilled beef carcasses being fed into the holds directly from the overhead gantries. But today it was stock-still and silent; although the derricks were swung out, clear of the hatches in deference to the speedier machinery - when the machinery happened to be working. A handful of deckies were on the fo'c'sle, chipping rust from around a hawsepipe, but that was the extent of activity.

Steve sauntered back to his cabin where Jim was now awake and perusing the columns of the Herald. 'You going ashore this afternoon?' asked Steve, mainly for the sake of conversation.

'Dunno. I might pop over to the Welcome bar,' answered the other lad, laying the paper aside and picking up his packet of Woodbines, 'but I'll be going to the Catholic later.'

'Well, if you're going over to the Welcome Bar I may as well join you,' replied Steve, firing up a Rothmans and blowing the smoke at the deck-head. 'I've got nothing spoiling - well, not this afternoon at any rate, although I've got a date with Lara this evening.'

'What! Without Helga keeping an eye on her? Well, that's a turn-up for the book,' declared Jim, raising a quizzical eyebrow, the look on his face betraying his obvious surprise. 'Lucky you. Where those girls are concerned she reckons she's their guardian angel.'

The Welcome Bar was lacking in custom; and whether or not it was because the abattoir was shut but there weren't so many flies about, either. There was a scattering of guys off the *Uruguay Star* and a couple of locals off a scow; but that was about it apart from Georgina and Charlotte who were sipping gin and orange in a corner. Charlotte, along with Connie and Eileen were Georgina's cabin-mates and between them they were a formidable foursome. Their capacity for booze was legendary and they'd carry on drinking, apparently sober, long after others were horizontal.

'What, supping on your own, girls?' chirped Jim, cheerfully, as he and Steve took their beers to the table and joined the two stewards who were heavily made-up and looked as if they were off to a party.

'Not now you two are here, Duckie,' answered Georgina, cheekily, crossing her legs in an exaggerated fashion and tucking her feet beneath her chair. 'We're off to a bash at the Copper Kettle as soon as Connie and Eileen get here - but they'll be ages so you're welcome to join us in the meantime.'

And so, they spent the next five hours in as fine a company as you could find - at least in this corner of the Welcome Bar. The conversation - most of it between Georgina and Charlotte while Steve and Jim did the listening - ranged between the invariably amusing via the occasionally catty to the downright horribly spiteful, especially when it featured other queens. Most of the jibes were aimed at their erstwhile shipmates, so what they couldn't hear wouldn't hurt them. But as Steve well knew, that was the nature of the type; girls will be girls and the *Sombrero's* quartet were no different. At one stage it became utterly ridiculous, when Charlotte led off about a steward called Sally with whom she'd sailed aboard Houlder's *Duquesa*. 'Talk about mutton dressed up as lamb,' she scoffed, as if slandering some middle-aged fashion model, 'she must have been fifty if she was a day.' Steve chuckled, but couldn't help noticing that beneath all the make-up, Charlotte must have been knocking on sixty.

And so the day wore inexorably on. The beer became rum and heads became muzzy; until in swayed Connie and Eileen, swinging their backsides - and that brought them up with a jolt. Connie, the youngest of the four, was a glamour-puss if ever there was one and she flaunted it brazenly. This afternoon, in addition to the carefully-

138

applied make-up, she wore a honey-blonde wig which covered her ears with a hair-line just below the collar. This, along with pink shirt and trousers was extremely eye catching; so with the large white gardenia that was pinned to the wig she could easily have passed for a film star.

'Christ! I could almost fancy her,' slurred Jim, who seldom spoke rashly and if sober wouldn't have uttered such rubbish. Not that it mattered in the slightest, Steve knowing very well it was just booze-driven piffle rather than a statement of intent.

And speaking of inebriation: Steve stared intently at his watch, striving to focus until he finally deciphered the time. It was past five o'clock and he ought to be shifting his carcase. 'Well, tha's me finished for the afternoon,' he slavered, rising waveringly and nearly tripping over his winklepickers. 'Whooops,' he quavered, grabbing Jim's shoulder to prevent himself crashing over sideways, 'mus've'ad a couple too many. Ne're mind - I'm gonna get ready to meet Lara. Bye, girls........seeyalater, Jim,' and with an unsteady gait he set a meandering course for the doorway.

'Bye, Duckie,' called Georgina, as Steve leant against the Jukebox, just to steady himself before resuming his mazy path doorwards. 'Don't do anything I wouldn't.' Steve raised a hand and stumbled out into the sunlight.

A couple too many was an understatement. In fact, Steve hadn't felt this bad in ages; well - not since that night in Recifé when he'd got slaughtered on the local cachaça. That's what you get for drinking on an empty stomach, he told himself, remembering that apart from that solitary roll he'd had nothing to eat since early the previous evening. Still, what was done was done; and seeing that in his present condition he couldn't have eaten even a single cream-cracker he reeled on until he reached the *Sombrero*.

Hauling himself up the accommodation ladder he was greeted by Barney, the gangway watchman, who'd been studying his antics with amusement. 'Hi, Steve - you all right, mate?' greeted Barney, who could see very well that Steve wasn't all right but instead looked downright, bloody awful.

'Nah, I feel as if I wanna throw up,' groaned Steve, who looked as green as a pea and in imminent danger of being sick.

'Oh! No! Not up here you don't,' rejoined Barney, who'd altered his tune in an instant and had visions of a mess to clean up. 'You get on down to them heads - and don't trip over that coaming.'

Steve didn't trip over the coaming, and made it to the heads with just seconds to spare before spewing up in a pan. It had been a close call, the only witness being Bob, the Third Cook, who was having a shave as Steve slammed the cubicle door. In fact, there wasn't that much to bring up - mostly what he'd recently drunk. After retching fruitless for about thirty seconds he flushed the toilet, sat down on the seat and was asleep before his head hit the bulkhead.

He was woken about two hours later, by a couple of stewards playing silly buggers, engaged in a water fight at the washbasins where they were supposed to be cleaning their teeth. He shook his head, took a glance at his watch and sat gazing at the cubicle door. And then the time on his watch-face registered; it read gone seven-thirty and he was due to meet Lara at eight. He leapt to his feet and immediately wished that he hadn't. His head was pounding and his tummy was churning but at least he no longer felt sick. He opened the cubicle door and the water fight abruptly ceased. Ignoring the mocking comments from Frank and Mark, a pair of saloon stewards who were renowned for their skylarking and mickey-taking, he stepped out of his clothes and into a shower in the hope of a rallying revival.

Dripping water and holding his clothes in front of him, he dawdled stark-bollock naked, back to his cabin in search of a couple of codeine. The shower, only luke-warm but refreshing, had partly done the job but codeine were the ultimate solution. This powerful panacea, so beloved by Mimi Gray - irreverently referred to as 'Codeine Annie' - sister in charge of the sick-bay back at the *Vindicatrix*, Steve knew was the be all and end all; if codeine didn't work then the evening was bound to be a washout.

But of course the codeine did the trick. They always did; and for this he'd be forever grateful to 'Codeine Annie' whose no-nonsense remedy over the previous three weeks had saved him immeasurable suffering. Within thirty minutes he was in a taxi, heading for nurses' home in the grounds of the Hospital Británico.

Lara had asked Steve to meet her at the nurses' home rather than the Flying Angel so as to avoid giving the impression she was a floozy. After all, a girl all alone in a place like that was bound to be the centre of attention. Whatever, he was hopelessly late and for that he'd have to apologise.

Steve's command of the Spanish language was indisputably woeful. That said, in little over a month he'd mastered sufficient to procure food and drink, and transport when the need had arisen. And so it was that he arrived at the foyer of the nurse's home which formed part of the hospital complex. However, ordering a 'café con leche' or a 'bifé de costilla' was kid's stuff compared with 'conversation'. His stuttering attempts to convey to the foyer receptionist that he'd like her to relay a message were greeted with a smile of amusement. She allowed him to ramble on, making a complete fool of himself; until she finally put him out of his misery by announcing, in perfect English, 'I'll give her a ring - and I'm sure she'll be down here directly.'

In fact, the receptionist knew all about Steve; well, as much as Lara had told her, as she and Lara had been busily gossiping while the latter was waiting for her date. When he hadn't arrived at the

141

appointed hour - nor twenty minutes later - she'd given up hope, believing he'd given her the elbow.

So Steve took a seat in the foyer while the receptionist, having made the phone call, sat tapping away at her typewriter. He felt an absolute dope; which of course he ought given that this was the British Hospital serving the British community among whom English was the everyday language. Buenos Aires was hugely cosmopolitan; and he should have known better, he reflected, when there was the French Hospital, the Italian Hospital, the Israeli Hospital and goodness-knows how many more hospitals, all serving their respective communities, employing their distinctive languages but where Spanish was the common-denominator.

But then his reverie was broken. The sound of high heels could be heard tripping along; and there was Lara, as stunningly beautiful as ever. 'Sorry I'm late,' he apologized, rising to his feet and greeting her with a kiss on the cheek. 'I'll explain while we're walking - but you'll have to excuse my embarrassment.' He'd no intention of laying a smokescreen; he was an implausible liar and she'd know straight away that he was making up tales as he went. And so, as they strolled through the Parque España he related how he'd had too much to drink and made himself ill before falling asleep in the toilet. That's what had made him late - that, and the need for a shower before making the dash to the hospital.

Lara thought it highly amusing, and wasn't at all angry that she'd been left in the lurch while Steve had been snoring in the loo. 'That'll teach you to drink more moderately,' she teased, unexpectedly linking her arm through his as they walked in the warm evening air towards wherever Lara had chosen. 'Too much alcohol spoils the liver - we learnt that today as part of our training. If people could see some of the pickled livers back there in the laboratory,' she added, nodding back over her shoulder in the direction of the hospital, 'they'd give up the drink altogether.'

And so they carried on, past Estación Constitución where you could catch a train to the coast, to Bahia Blanca, Viedma and even to points further south. They crossed the broad expanse of the Avenida 9 de Julio, through a warren of alleys until they came to the Calle Humberto. Here they entered a high-ceilinged restaurant festooned with crystal chandeliers. It had brown-panelled walls and marble-tiled floors; a shining example of class and expense that only the wealthy might frequent. Solid-silver cutlery, snow-white tablecloths and linen serviettes all added to the aura of opulence and Steve saw his Pesos evaporating.

But that wasn't the case by any means. A bife de costella, with a glass of red wine was extraordinarily modestly priced. Lara chose the same, insisting as always that she foot her own bill although she accepted a drink when Steve offered. As they ploughed through their steaks - Steve having completely forgotten Dick's gruesome portrayal of the abattoir - Lara related how she was in fact a student nurse while Helga was a fully-fledged sister; hence the impression that she was the other girls' guardian. Lara, it transpired was the youngest of the four, hoping to pass her exams in the forthcoming months and join Kari and Marianela on the wards. But for the present she spent most her time in the classroom with spells on the wards as part of her ongoing training. Tonight, she explained, barring exceptional circumstances, would be the last time they'd meet as for the rest of the week she'd be learning her trade on the night-shift.

As the evening slipped by their relationship blossomed; and when Lara took hold of Steve's hand, saying how much she liked him, how she hoped that he'd write and how perhaps they could meet up in future, he felt smugly elated. He replied in kind, saying very much the same while extolling her beauty and kindness. Yes, he'd certainly keep in touch; and yes, provided he returned this way - although he explained that this was something he couldn't be sure of - they could certainly rekindle their friendship. As they left the restaurant and made their unhurried way back to the hospital Lara laid her head on his shoulder. This was something else he wasn't prepared for - any more than he was prepared for the 'finale'.

As they walked through the Parque España they passed beneath a tree where Lara paused and unzipped her handbag. She produced a wafer-thin packet that Steve, looking puzzled, mistook for a stick of chewing-gum. But it wasn't chewing-gum at all. Lara had come fully prepared, and without waiting for Steve to pose unnecessary questions she dragged him into the shrubs where their passion was enveloped by the night.

Christ! They're never going to believe me, he mused, as he crossed the Puente Nicolás Avellaneda and down on to the dusty track that led to the quayside and eventually back to the *Sombrero*. Those girls are supposed to be paragons of virtue; hadn't Helga said as much when she'd related how she'd almost ruined the future of a Liverpool lad who'd molested her in the back of a taxi? Best to keep quiet, he reflected, and enjoy the secret as he knew it. The grin on his face said it all; but didn't distract him from the shadows which always posed a threat at this time of night, especially for those walking solo. But there, he'd soon be back at the quayside and back at the quayside there were soldiers. But on rounding the corner of the Anglo there wasn't a soldier in sight. Instead, there was the solitary marinero, performing his lonely police duties. And there was something else that was different - the sound of activity at the Anglo whereas for the previous two days there'd been nothing.

'The strike's over - they've gone back to work,' announced Graham who'd taken over the duties of gangway watchman from Barney. 'They started back on the night-shift.'

The *Sombrero*, it appeared, would soon resume loading and it wouldn't come a second too soon. You see, although refrigerated the cargo of beef wasn't frozen. Rather, it was chilled, in order that its freshly-butchered qualities were preserved. It had to be shipped to a tight schedule to avoid being spoilt so was as important if not more so than the mail. The strike had caused a lengthy delay and haste was now of the essence.

When Steve turned to in the morning he was grinning like a Cheshire cat; he just couldn't help it following his romp in the bushes with Lara.

'Why are you looking so pleased with yourself?' queried Jim, who'd spent a rather sedate evening in the company of Sister Teresa at the Catholic Mission where there'd been nothing more stimulating than a darts match, 'You seem as happy as a dog with two tails.'

You can say that again, thought Steve, who'd made up his mind that knowledge of the frolic was his affair only and not to be freely circulated. 'Oh! Nothing - just thoughts,' he answered, evasively, trying his darnedest to keep a straight face as Jim looked perplexed, trying to unravel the enigma. Jim was no fool, but he'd never guess the truth about this one.

And Steve had no intention of telling him as he set off to work, in the gleaming main galley that had become such a pleasure to work in. What a contrast, he thought, with the crew galley aft that was almost prehistoric by comparison. As already noted, the main galley was totally enclosed but it was spotless and bright with no trace of coal dust or smoke. Working clockwise from the large sink and drainer - which was located immediately forward of the officers' and engineers' servery - it was largely rectangular with stainless-steel worktops bordering the perimeter as far as the domestic refrigerators. Then came the galley entrance; wide open at present but shuttered and locked overnight. Beyond the entrance -

alongside which Frederico Henrique had his diminutive pantry - were the butcher's and bakers' shops while further on still, ranging along the remaining bulkheads and almost completing the rectangle were the, chip-maker, food-mixer, rumbler, salamander and steamer. The square was finally rounded adjacent to the servery by a bulbous-bottomed, galvanized boiler. The boiler, powered by electricity and resembling a cauldron, had a handy fifty-gallon capacity. Back at the 'Vindi' almost identical vessels had been utilized for boiling the potatoes, cabbage and other vegetables. Not so aboard the *Sombrero*. Her galley boiler was used solely for either mixing up sugi, dhobying pantry cloths or for boiling the grease out of mutton cloth (The cotton shrouds in which carcasses of meat are clothed prior to leaving the abattoir). This latter was then cut into lengths and used as dusters, strapping-up cloths or whatever.

And so, what of the remaining deck space? Well, the galley centrepiece was an electric stove that glistened like a newly - built Cadillac. Set into the surface were sixteen hotplates in clusters of four that in turn sat square above the ovens. Over the stove and suspended from the deck-head was a trough-shaped canopy that in a domestic kitchen would generally be referred to as a 'cooker-hood'. Set into this canopy were a bank of extractor fans which lifted steam and cooking odours clear of the galley to be exhausted via the *Sombrero's* forward funnel. In the absence of air-conditioning, ventilation was courtesy of the ubiquitous Punka-louvres of which the galley was generously endowed.

It was in this sparkling environment that Steve had fed spuds through the 'rumbler' and was now slicing them ready for the saucepan. Back in the antiquated crew galley, with his hand-held peeler, it would have taken forever to peel the day's quota of potatoes; but thanks to the main galley's superior technology the entire operation, including the slicing, was completed in less than twenty minutes. But of course, as he already knew, up-to-date

146

methods didn't always equate to a sinecure. They couldn't possibly; not with the number of mouths to feed, three times a day and in the evenings if a barbecue was scheduled. He'd seen quite sufficient during the outward-bound voyage to convince him of the tremendous workload. Indeed, if it wasn't for the various modern innovations then coping wouldn't be feasible. He supposed that in years gone by, before the advent of labour-saving appliances, extra staff would have been an absolute necessity.

But that was then and this was today when the job was a comparative pushover. That said, he knew very well that in forty-eight hours he'd be desperate to escape the frenzy. And then of course, there was Whisky. Okay, the animal was happy - it'd be a surprise if he wasn't what with all the fussing he was getting - but it'd be nice to get back to normal, himself, Michael and the cat; that's assuming the moggy didn't harbour a grudge and slope off back to the mess-room. But he'd worry about that when the time came. For the present, there were more pressing issues, all of them wrapped up in money.

For instance, Jim had suggested that tomorrow, their final day off, they take a trip out to Tigre, a river resort about twenty miles north of the capital. 'I don't know,' wavered Steve, who'd been fretting about the state of his finances although it sounded like an excellent day out. 'I'm down to less than three-hundred Pesos and I still haven't bought any presents.' He'd changed his remaining Pound note the previous evening, at a cambio on the Avenida Caseros. He'd left it late in the day in order to obtain the best exchange rate. This was owing to the astronomical rate of inflation which caused exchange values to fluctuate - invariably upwards - by the minute. He could have waited indefinitely, but he hadn't known how much he might need for his fabulous night out with Lara.

'How much Sterling have you actually got left?' asked Jim, formulating a plan that might allow Steve to partake of a trip out to

Tigre yet still afford presents for his family. 'You must have some coins in your pockets.'

'Just over sixteen shillings - a ten-bob note and some change,' answered Steve, wondering what Jim was angling at.

'Well, there you are then. That's got to be worth something - more than enough for your train fare to Tigre with plenty left over for other things - and you'll still have your three-hundred Pesos, or whatever it is.'

'But where am I going to exchange it?' queried Steve, who knew very well that cambios didn't deal in shillings and pence - only in base currency units. 'I'm not a magician.'

'Don't you worry about that,' reassured Jim, who knew just the man who might help solve Steve's monetary dilemma. 'When we go ashore I'll introduce you to your benefactor.'

Hmmm........sounds promising, thought Steve, just so long as it doesn't involve criminality, like selling ship's stores for instance. He was determined to avoid that at all costs. He knew very well it went on; deckhands selling paint, rope and goodness-knows-what while firemen flogged anything that moved. Among the catering staff it was a poorly-kept secret that some supplemented their subs by touting all manner of provisions, even joints of meat and poultry. But there was always the risk of getting caught. Alan for one had already been in trouble after trying to sell a sack of potatoes. The transaction itself had gone smoothly. The trouble arose when the purchaser, an Anglo employee, had tried quite blatantly to carry it ashore in the full glare of daylight without looking over his shoulder. If the gangway watchman had been on his own then he might have succeeded. As it was the Second Mate, who just happened to be chatting with Barney, spotted what was afoot and hauled the fellow up in his tracks. The spuds were returned to their locker, the would-be buyer - who according to him - believed he'd negotiated a legitimate purchase, had his money refunded while Alan was cautioned and was fortunate not to have been reported. However, there was nothing shady about Jim's proposal as Steve discovered later that evening.

As was often the case given the organization's Anglican roots, the Superintendent at the Mission was an Englishman, a native of Nottingham in this instance. His name was Andy, he was about thirty years old and according to all accounts he was an accomplished badminton player. However, he wasn't playing badminton this evening. 'How much have you actually got?' he asked, when Jim explained Steve's predicament.

'Sixteen and tuppence-ha'penny,' answered Steve, rummaging about in his pocket and coming up with a fistful of change. 'There's a ten-bob note, quite a bit of silver and the odd tuppence-ha'penny in coppers.'

'Well, let me see,' answered Andy, as he made a rough calculation before announcing what he was prepared to offer. 'Tell you what, does three-hundred Pesos sound reasonable?'

'It most certainly does,' replied Steve, surprised at the man's generosity as he handed over the change and pocketed a bundle of banknotes. 'But tell me, what on earth do you want with a pocketful of shrapnel? You'll not be able to spend it over here.'

'No, but I will be able to at home. You see, I'm returning to the UK in January - just temporarily, mind you, to see my mum and dad and the rest of the family, and to get married as it happens. The change is bound to come in handy.'

In the course of the ensuing conversation it transpired that the Superintendent, an ordained priest although he seldom wore a collar, would be sailing aboard the *Arlanza,* a spanking new passenger-cargo liner that flew the colours of the Royal Mail. By that he meant the Royal Mail Line shipping company - not Royal Mail as in 'Post Office'. It also emerged that when he returned to BA he'd be bringing his wife along with him. Steve also suspected that the man had come to his financial assistance, not because he needed a pocketful of 'groats' but purely out of the goodness of his heart.

So, what about those presents for his family. Well, now was the best time to buy them, while he had money in his pockets so that whatever was left would be his to dispose of as he pleased. It was in this happy frame of mind that with his friends for company he crossed Cochabamba and entered the bounteous souvenir shop. But what should he purchase given the plethora of 'goodies' on offer? Well, his brother was easy; a black-and-white cow-skin belt with a large silvery buckle seemed the obvious answer - although whether his brother would be equally smitten would later be a matter of conjecture. Maybe a scarf for his mum and a pair of cuff-links for his dad? But then he spotted something special - a calf-skin handbag at only a hundred Pesos but in a class of its own by any standard. And the cuff-links for his dad? Why not - and a pair for himself into the bargain. So at two-hundred Pesos he felt quietly content as Mary placed his goods in a bag. He waited while his pals paid for their own purchases; then having tendered their thanks they were about to leave the shop when Charlie appeared, and asked, 'What are you gentlemen doing for the rest of the evening? Do you fancy a trip around town?'

And so it was that the four of them, with Charlie as chauffeur, embarked on a landmark tour of Buenos Aires in an oversized slope-backed Buick that smoothed out the cobbles as if they'd been freshly-laid tarmac.

The true purpose for the mission was so that Charlie could deliver some items to a customer at Palermo who wished to distribute them as Christmas gifts. In the course of their journey they passed through swanky Recoleta, arguably the city's most affluent district and home to the world-renowned cemetery. Recoleta cemetery, a virtual 'City of the Dead', a 'home from home' for the departed, was where the remains of the wealthy lay in fine mausoleums that reflected their station in society. In later years it also provided a final resting place for the much-revered Eva Perón, the fabled Evita, patron of the poor and wife of Juan Perón, the former Argentine president. After her embalmed body was returned to Argentina from Europe following her husband's enforced exile she was eventually laid to rest in the Duarte (her maiden name) family tomb, arguably the grandest of them all. Almost overnight the tomb became a shrine where her devotees came in droves, to worship their champion while others indulged their curiosity.

It appears that following her death at the age of thirty-three in July 1952, Eva's body led a chequered existence. Following a lying in state - an unusual event in itself given that she was merely the president's spouse - it was initially displayed in the congress building where it remained while its fate was decided. However, in 1955, before such plans could be finalized, Juan Perón was displaced by a military coup which saw him flee Argentina, leaving the cadaver in limbo. Throughout the years of the ensuing dictatorship Perónism was banned, and it was during this period that the embalmed corpse disappeared. It was only in 1971 that the military revealed that the body was buried in Milan, but how it had arrived there was a mystery. Whatever, the remains were exhumed and transported to Spain where the Perón family then resided. In 1973 Juan Perón came out of exile and returned to Argentina where he again assumed the role of president. He died in office in 1974 and his then wife, Isobel, whom he'd married in 1961 and who succeeded him as president, had Eva's body repatriated and subsequently interred at Recoleta.

And so their tour continued, through leafy Belgrano; sedate Chacarita; middle-class Villa Crespo; stylish Balvanera and back to

151

Retiro before a grand finale along the Avenida 9 de Julio. Charlie dropped them off at the bridge from where they strolled to the ship, having thanked him for the spin in his Buick. As they dawdled through the dust Steve wondered at the warmness of the Argentine people; that was discounting, of course, the obvious rougher faction of whom they'd had first-hand experience. Perhaps where Charlie was concerned it was simply a matter of fostering customer relations, although both he and his wife were unquestionably kind and would go out of their way to be friendly.

Their trip out to Tigre was exhilarating, although it might never have happened had circumstances been less problematic. It was during the journey that Jim revealed that he'd originally considered a day out at Mar del Plata, a fashionable resort on the shores of the South Atlantic. But after consulting a map and the relevant railway timetable he'd concluded that it just wasn't practical. By the time they arrived it would be time to return and thus a waste of good time and money. And so Tigre it was, and an inspired choice it was too.

The place was a breath of fresh air after the polluted and traffic-clogged capital. Being a weekday it was peaceful, with just a handful of trippers enjoying their ease in the mysterious heartland of the delta. Jim had hinted that Tigre was comparable with Henley-on-Thames back in Oxfordshire; a passable description as the abundance of boat-houses testified - although there was much more to Tigre than river-sport and millionaires' junkets.

In fact, the delta of the Rio Paraná comprised a profusion of jungle-clad channels, the three principle watercourses in the immediate vicinity being the rivers Tigre, Luján and Sarmiento. The island-strewn wetlands could be easily explored by taking a boat trip from Tigre, and the boat fare didn't cost a fortune. On some of the islands there were hotels and restaurants where the well-to-do squandered their money while luxuriating in the delta's solitude. And then of course there was the wildlife, invariably rich but more bountiful at present than ever. You see, over the previous weeks there'd been exceptional rain over the Bolivian and Brazilian rainforests. This had led to the rivers becoming swollen; and this was reflected in the large clumps of foliage that could be seen floating by on their way to the estuary and the sea. But clumps of vegetation wasn't all, because clinging to the greenery there were creatures of all sorts, mammals in excess while snakes and amphibians abounded. It was a scene that was rarely repeated; probably as well from the animals' perspective given that their future seemed far from assured. But that was nature in the raw and there was little if anything that humanity could do to forestall it.

But back to the area itself. Prior to becoming a magnet for tourists, the islands especially had been a flourishing fruit-growing centre, the produce being shipped just a few miles downriver to the capital. A vestige of that industry was still to be seen with a variety of fruit trees lining the riverbanks and pavements. Jim related that in the course of an earlier trip, during the fruit-ripening season, he'd gorged on what he'd assumed were either enormous raspberries or oversized, under-ripe blackberries; that was despite being warned on countless occasions never to eat anything he didn't recognize. It had later emerged that the fruit that he'd eaten had in fact been mulberries, which probably accounted for the sweeter than anticipated taste.

The Paraná delta is an area of outstanding natural beauty, a lush cornucopia less than an hour away from one of the world's most energetic cities. It is revered by some as being one of the most wondrous places on earth while others simply liken it to the Amazon, which to many would be praise enough. A day-excursion was nowhere nearly sufficient to thoroughly explore the region which is almost the size of Wales. Nevertheless, to have been there at all was a privilege that wouldn't be forgotten in a hurry.

Upon their return to the city Jim retired to the company of Sister Teresa - an arrangement that was occurring increasingly frequently causing many to question his motives - while Steve spent an hour at Retiro, either watching the trains or sampling a beer in the buffet.

The following morning there was chaos, at least for a while, putting the prospect of breakfast in jeopardy. 'What's happened here, then?' asked Steve, when he arrived at the galley to find it in darkness and as silent as an overgrown churchyard.

'Fuckin' lights have all fused,' swore Derek, as he groped his way around until he discovered the switch panel which was located adjacent to the bakery.

A couple of lights were usually left on overnight for security reasons, enabling the watchman to peer through the grill in the roller-shutter. Rather surprisingly, when he'd woken them the watchman hadn't mentioned anything about the galley lights being out which suggested he hadn't been doing his job properly.

'Probably a short-circuit, or maybe condensation in the switch panel,' offered Derek, throwing each of the switches in turn in the forlorn hope that the lights might suddenly illuminate. But it wasn't just the lights. The fans wouldn't work and the fridges were already defrosting so electrical assistance was called for.

'I'm not surprised you can't see anything,' reported the Chief Electrician, from the top of a stepladder while examining the fuse-box which was sited above the galley doorway, 'someone's swiped all the fuses.'

'What? Who the hell would want to nick the fuses?' queried Derek, of no-one in particular as he furrowed his brow and fired up a Senior Service. 'They'd be no use to anyone - I bet someone's pinched them for a lark.'

154

'They've more than likely been flogged,' volunteered Michael, as a more plausible alternative, quickly appreciating that as industrial fuses they'd be worth a small fortune to the trade.

'That's the most logical answer,' agreed the Chief Electrician, who'd descended his stepladder and was about to go in search of replacements. 'Sell anything, some blokes, if they thought it'd buy a drop of grog.'

Another ten minutes then the lights were ablaze and breakfast was sizzling in the pan. 'I tell you,' started the electrician, to an attentive audience as he packed away his gear in his tool-box, 'several years ago I was 'Second Leccy' on a tramp. We were in Kingston, Jamaica, at the time and me and the Chief were rewiring a cabinet in the wheelhouse. Anyway, we'd forgotten to lock the door to our workshop, and when we got back it'd been stripped - you know, a couple of extension leads, a reel of copper wiring, a soldering iron, not to mention a bagful of tools. We swore at ourselves for not locking the door because we should have known better with that crew. I tell you, they were a right bunch of bastards - and as for making money. They'd sell their own sisters for a snifter. The Chief suspected the shore gang but I'd've bet my life on the deckies - and you know what? When I rummaged through their mess-room there it all was - in the hot-press, waiting to be smuggled ashore. Well, there you are - everything's fixed and I've padlocked the fuse box so that should put a stop to the thieving. I'll label the key and keep it somewhere safe so we'll know where to find it in future.'

That evening there was a party in the Welcome Bar, a farewell extravaganza laid on by the splendid Georgina. In fact, it was more akin to a nightclub revue as the crew were entertained by the *Sombrero's* most glamorous 'cuties'. As expected, Connie was the star with a sultry impression of Marlena Deitrich singing 'Falling in

Love Again' to a piano accompaniment played by a smoke-room steward. Not to be outdone, Faye, one of the queens off the *Uruguay Star* did a striptease, right down to a skimpy pair of knickers; and was only prevented from removing the lot by the bar-owner on the grounds of 'propriety'.

The only sour note was when Charlotte got thumped for touching up a fireman whom she'd mistakenly thought might have fancied her. It could have turned nasty but the guy was restrained; and once the tears had dried up and Charlotte had reapplied her make-up he bought her a gin and they ended up dancing a cha-cha.

And so drew to a close Steve's first ever visit to Buenos Aires - and what a stupendous initiation. But now it was coming to an end. Tomorrow the *Sombrero* would be sailing and it would be back to the grindstone; or as near to the grindstone as he was likely to get in the unhurried world of their galley.

Looking back over the days since their arrival Steve recalled how earlier in the year he hadn't wanted to leave New Zealand; now here he was in another part of the world, wishing he could stay in Argentina. But in New Zealand the situation had been different. Way back in the South Pacific he'd been desperately in love with Maxine - a relationship that still endured - and he still couldn't wait to return, whereas here in BA it had been a continuous sequence of merrymaking with just the occasional more temperate interlude.

As they made their way back to the *Sombrero* it suddenly occurred that he'd been so preoccupied with enjoying himself that he'd badly neglected his letter writing. It was something he'd have to redress and the sooner he got started the better. His family would come first as always and then he'd have to write to his grandmother; an air-letter each at least - but then he'd have to think about Maxine. He knew it would fill several pages, telling of his adventures and the places he'd been and of some of the people he'd encountered. He'd tell about Lisbon and Rio and all about crazy BA. In fact, he'd have so much to say he wouldn't really know where to start; but he'd manage it somehow - conveniently omitting that unbelievable night out with Lara.

12

The following morning found Steve and Michael in the familiar surroundings of the crew galley which was thankfully much as they'd left it. Despite its shortcomings it was great to be back, although there'd be no modern wizardry to make life that little less irksome. Upon unlocking the port-side half-doors it had been a pleasant surprise to find everything neat, clean and tidy. The first job was to light up the fire so that the stove would be hot enough for frying. The foundations were laid using newspaper and finely-chopped kindling topped off with a shovelful of coal. A match was then applied and a sheet of newspaper stretched across the front of the fire-grill. This induced rapid combustion, sucking in air from below so that in no time at all the hot-plates were glowing like lanterns.

As the fire took a hold then Michael began writing out his stores list which would be virtually identical to the one he'd compiled back in London. Once the list was complete it would be handed to Steve who for the present was otherwise engaged.

'Hello, Matey,' greeted Steve, as he squatted down and stroked Whisky's head before caressing the fur along his spine. 'Have you missed me? You shouldn't have. I've been to see you as often as I could and made sure you've had plenty of tucker.' The cat raised his head, inviting Steve to tickle his chin before rolling over to have his belly rubbed.

'He's been as good as gold,' said Graham, who'd entered the mess-room and was pouring out a bowlful of 'Kellogg's. 'Okay, he's disappeared occasionally - you know, out on the prowl and so on, and we know for a fact he's been ashore. But he's been fussed something rotten, especially by the peggy as something in the way of a "thank you". Anyway - fancy a cuppa while you're down here?'

'No thanks - I've gotta get back,' answered Steve, carefully lifting the now battered box, moggy included, and heading for the galley companionway. 'I've got to fetch the stores, peel the spuds and attend to a cart-load of other chores. But you know what? This spell in BA has been a cakewalk - and I don't mind admitting that work'll come hard in the short term.'

'You don't say,' ribbed Graham, who'd seldom been ashore as a result of the watch-keeping rota. 'Life's a bloody breeze for some folk.'

Steve grinned. 'Well, thanks for looking after him,' he acknowledged, nodding at Whiskey who was now sitting erect and surveying the mess-room around him. 'It was good to know he was being cared for.'

The stores took an hour to collect - two separate journeys; half the length of the ship whereas for the previous ten days he'd only had to pop around the corner. At first he joined the queue at the dry stores where the grumpy Second Steward had a cob on. 'That's right, all come at fuckin' once,' he complained, as the pantries, dining rooms and mess-rooms stocked up for the homeward-bound passage, 'I'll be open again first-thing tomorrow.'

'We need the stuff now,' retorted Frank, who was renowned for his cheek, Second Steward or no Second Steward. 'You've had fuck all to do since we got here so the exercise'll do you fuckin' good.' The queue laughed *en masse* and the Second Steward fumed but he knew he'd get his own back in the long run.

The queue gradually shortened and as Steve reached the front he was expecting a dig about Michael. But no, rather surprisingly Sec rambled on about how if he didn't get the stores closed in double-quick time he'd be lucky if he got any breakfast. But then Steve recalled an occurrence, earlier in the week when the stores hadn't opened till lunchtime. Aha! he thought, the reason he hasn't mentioned Michael and started prattling on about his breakfast is a crafty attempt at diverting attention from his own sins. You see, it wasn't so much that Sec had been sloshed as the fact that he'd been absolutely 'blotto'. It had apparently happened in the bond locker where he was supposedly carrying out some stocktaking; quite literally so it appeared, as after over-imbibing he'd been dragged to his cabin by a couple of deckies who'd found him flaked out near the swimming pool. Fortunately the Purser hadn't known - he'd conveniently been away on a hunting trip - and the stewards had functioned unsupervised. Hmmm, reasoned Steve, a grin on his face almost as wide as the River Plate estuary - talk about kettles and pots.

It was whilst executing the second part of his errand - collecting the meats and dairy produce - that the Butcher relayed that the homeward-bound calls at both Montevideo and Recifé had been cancelled owing to the delay at the Anglo. 'Came from the Purser's own lips,' declared the Butcher, a fellow from Ramsgate called Martin who wasn't at all happy with the arrangement. 'Bit of a bastard, that is. There's a bird I was gonna meet in Recifé - now it'll have to wait until next trip.'

Martin's 'bird in Recifé' had been a talking point since goodness-knows when. This was his fourteenth trip on the ship and throughout that time he'd always referred to Maria as his 'girlfriend'. The trouble was, Martin was a self-deluded fool; because everyone knew that Maria was a whore and a very high class one at that. How much it was costing him was guesswork but it must have been hideously expensive. Almost everyone thought he was nuts, especially when a ten-minute bang with a scrubber near the docks could be had for the price of a Bacardi. But how he spent his money was his business so who were others to pour scorn?

Anyway, the galley telegraph was transmitting with its usual exactitude and news soon got around that the calls at both Montevideo and Recifé had indeed been excluded in an attempt to recover the timetable. The handful of passengers that should have been boarding at 'Monty' were being flown to BA and the *Sombrero* would be sailing at noon. This was confirmed by a blackboard at the head of the accommodation ladder that also notified that shore-leave would expire at eleven.

So, what of the cargo and mail that was due to be transferred at the ports that were now off her schedule. Well, the *Uruguay Star* would be following; and seeing that the Blue Star Line also had a contract with the Post Office the 'Star boat' would accommodate the mail. And as for the cargo; another of the Simpson Line's freighters, the *Cucurucho*, which was currently loading in Fray Bentos, would take care of whatever was on offer.

Shortly before their departure a DBS from the Lamport & Holt liner *Defoe* was placed aboard for repatriation to Britain. Apparently, he'd spent the past three weeks in the Hospital Británico suffering the effects of pneumonia. Although not yet fully recovered he was considered fit enough to travel and the *Sombrero* was providing his passage. Although he didn't know it, he'd be joined in Santos by another 'castaway', this one from Houlder's *Condesa*. However, this fellow's circumstances would be different. He'd been hauled from the gutter in the city's red-light district long after the *Condesa* had sailed.

And so, shortly after twelve, with tugs fore and aft, the *Sombrero* took her leave of Buenos Aires, inching away from the wharf and towards the Rio Riachuelo. In order to minimize delay the call at Puerto Nuevo had been waived, the passengers boarding instead in the unwholesome surroundings of the Anglo. They must have

161

wondered where they were heading as the fleet of coaches trundled along the quay before drawing to a halt at the abattoir. In a hopeless attempt at creating a semblance of decorum, the covered gangway usually employed for embarking passengers had been transported round from Puerto Nuevo, so at least while they were boarding the eyesore was temporarily obscured. However one thing that couldn't be hidden was the virtual absence of on-lookers. Earlier in the year, when the *Alice Springs* had sailed from ports in New Zealand, the wharves had been thronged with heartbroken, hanky-waving females. Here in BA, by contrast, the quay was deserted, with only the casting-off party and the lonely marinero to witness the *Sombrero's* departure.

Progress was initially slow, owing in no small measure to the ancient and unladen *Juncal* which was swinging in the fairway on her way to load oil at the tank farm. But it was a manoeuvre to which the vessel was accustomed, and she was soon clear of the river thus allowing the *Sombrero* to proceed. It wasn't long before the *Sombrero* herself was free of the Rio Riachuelo; only in her case it was into the more exposed waters of the Plate where a covering of cloud was being hastened by a stiffening breeze.

'Looks very much like a Pampero,' said the Lamp-trimmer, glancing at the sky as Steve emptied slops down the rubbish chute, 'I was wondering if we'd cop one of those.'

'What's a Pampero?' enquired Steve, whose interest in meteorology had yet to encompass some of the world's lesser-known phenomena. This is the first I've heard about it.'

'It's a squall system that blows up from either southern Patagonia or the Andes,' replied the 'Lampy', who was hunching his shoulders against the sudden chill that had materialized in an instant from nowhere. 'It can be bloody nasty at times, causing damage and often even worse.'

Steve could believe it. The muddy waters of the Plate, so often as smooth as a looking-glass, were already being whipped into abnormally large waves that slapped against the *Sombrero's* hull-plates. He too was now feeling the cold so he hurried into the warmth of the galley where Michael had already shut the doors.

'It was blowing through here like a hurricane,' said the cook, who also appeared to be an expert on everything Pampero. 'Mind you, the further north they get they usually blow themselves out although BA seems uncannily prone. But there,' he continued, as Steve felt a shiver and moved a little closer to the fire, 'the locals often welcome them warmly - especially in the summer when they counteract the heat and humidity.'

And so, with the Pampero cutting a path through her aerials and rigging the *Sombrero* proceeded on her course; passing smoky La Plata then Montevideo before meeting the lively Atlantic. By this time Steve was asleep, a dreamless sleep, the propensity for nightmares overcome. And as for the shooting incident - a catalyst for nightmares by anyone's reckoning - when Steve had first mentioned it to both Derek and Michael on the morning following, neither had the slightest recollection.

13

It was 7.00am on their second day out of Buenos Aires. As was ever the case in this part of the world the sun was shining although the air felt fresher than of late. This was probably owing to the after-effects of the Pampero that had swept on its way leaving the sea a little choppier than usual. Later tomorrow - weather permitting - or perhaps early the following morning the *Sombrero* would be tying up in Santos. Such a short passage would more often than not prove tedious, with nothing specific to write home about; but forty-eight hours was more than sufficient for the extraordinary to make itself known.

The first leapt out of the blue - quite literally - as Steve was about to dump the ashes. Rather than a 'bang' it was more of a near-silent 'thud', and the *Sombrero* shook, as if she'd run up on a sandbank. Fearing a collision or worse Steve dropped his bucket and dashed outside to the taffrail. He'd been half expecting to find his ship either aground or disabled; but no, she was still plugging along at her steady old eighteen knots. But then, frighteningly, breaking surface almost beneath him and almost scaring him to death rose a colossal black shape, soaring upwards before spiralling down, exposing a fluke-shaped tail.

'Whale!' exclaimed Michael, 'and a bloody great big one at that.' The cook had joined Steve at the rail and was pointing roughly at the spot where the beast had submerged in the hope that it might reappear. But no, it didn't re-emerge and that was the last they saw of it - vanished in the twinkle of an eye. By this time a considerable crowd had gathered, in the after well-deck and along the two promenade decks; but by now there was nothing to be seen and gradually the huddles dispersed. Meanwhile, the *Sombrero* forged on, doubtless with a few strained rivets while the unfortunate whale was almost certainly nursing a headache.

And then there was Gerry, a steward from Tyneside who was both mentally deficient and dishonest - except to those who didn't know him. Into this latter category fell a hapless apprentice engineer, when Gerry approached him and asked if he could borrow a hacksaw. Gerry explained that having misplaced the key he needed the hacksaw to saw through the padlock on his locker. Ever willing to oblige, the apprentice not only provided a hacksaw but offered to cut through the padlock, an offer that was readily accepted. Sadly, the locker wasn't Gerry's, belonging instead to a utility steward who on returning to his cabin found his locker door ajar and his wallet as empty as a vacuum. In the course of the ensuing investigation it was quickly established what had happened and who was responsible, with Gerry claiming he'd been drinking and hadn't known what he was thinking of. The trainee engineer - who by now felt an absolute dope - alleged the opposite, stating that Gerry had been sober and had spun such a yarn that he'd believed him without asking questions. Whatever, the incident was logged and the money returned although at that stage no action was taken, the Captain weighing up his options. However, the very least that Gerry could expect would be a fine and a detrimental (Decline to Report) discharge; whilst in the worst-case scenario he could be facing a gaol sentence.

The entire episode had been a classic example of a nincompoop out of his depth, if only for the muddle-headed belief that he actually thought he could have got away with it. And as for the dishonesty: well, everyone knew about Gerry; everyone, it seemed, apart from the apprentice engineer. Put simply, the steward was a 'tea-leaf' who couldn't be entrusted with shirt button.

In the event, following a brief call at Santos it was discovered that the Captain's options had been abrogated. Gerry, you see - despite no shore-leave being granted - had skinned out under the cover of darkness, carrying only a handful of possessions. It seemed that homelessness in Brazil was more attractive than a prison cell in Britain.

If the stopover at Santos had been brief then that at Rio was ephemeral; and not only that but the Skipper had again denied shore-leave - a decision that was roundly deplored. 'Can't even get ashore for a drink,' bemoaned Michael, eyeing up the bars in the distance, 'I bet this is all down to Gerry.'

Of course it was nothing of the sort. It was simply a case of the Captain needing to know that when it was time to depart he'd have sufficient crew to sail the ship. He was thinking specifically of the firemen. They'd caused enough trouble already; men being adrift when they should have been at work - so for the present he was taking no chances.

They left Rio in the late afternoon, slipping past some of the most fabulous scenery on earth, out into the Atlantic Ocean. It was then that they learnt of a change to their revamped itinerary. Their next scheduled port would be Teneriffe, followed by a brief call at Lisbon before completing the voyage back in London. However, a radio message from the Simpson Line's owners instructed that having recouped the lost time they should call additionally at Madeira, to embark a consignment of cork. Steve had never visited the island and was highly delighted at the prospect. Up until then he'd only associated Madeira with a variety of fortified wine and a delicious kind of cake that his mum made.

Now then, the legality or otherwise of marriage at sea has often been a bone of contention. The issue seems never to have been settled with some claiming such ceremonies are perfectly lawful while others say positively not. But whatever the arguments, marriage at sea has often proved popular with Hollywood so what happened on the evening of their departure from Rio might possibly have been worthy of an 'Oscar'. Given the opaqueness surrounding the issue the legitimacy was highly questionable, but two couples were spliced with the Captain administering the rites. The pairings were of opposite extremes; a twosome of youngsters who'd only recently met and a pair of widowed pensioners on holiday. But of one thing they could be absolutely certain: a record of the nuptials was entered in the log and each couple was handed a certificate. So, with credentials as proof they could each tell a real-life fairy tale.

The following morning it was business as usual; until around ten o'clock when the Chief Refrigerating Officer, who was carrying out maintenance, discovered a stowaway hiding in a fan room. With no means of escape the stranger surrendered and was taken to the Captain for interview. It soon became known that the man was of Italian origin, and that he'd boarded at Rio while the gangway was briefly unattended. Desperate for a return to Italy his intention had been to hide himself away until the *Sombrero* reached Lisbon from where he could thumb a lift overland to Genoa. Unfortunately for him he'd been rumbled.

Some thirty hours later the *Sombrero* rendezvoused with the *Montero* which was outward-bound for Buenos Aires. A considerable crowd had gathered as she drifted within hailing distance of her 'stable-mate'. A little later one of the lifeboats was lowered and the distraught stowaway, seeing his lifeline disappear, began his voyage back to Rio and the possibility of detention. Steve, who'd been studying the proceedings as intently as anyone, felt sympathy for the man as did most of those around him. He hoped that at some stage, if the fellow managed to escape custody, he'd stow away again and next time happily succeed.

And so they steamed on across the Atlantic, between the bulges of Brazil and West Africa before passing Cape Verde, *en route* to their stopover at Teneriffe. As on the outward passage the awning was proving invaluable, a funnel for cooling fresh air as well as a screen against sunburn. It was the same at the after end of the lower promenade deck where the awning had been re-erected, having been dismantled at the Anglo to enable the handling of cargo. Indeed, the living was easy; the weather was grand, his job was a breeze and the *Sombrero* was on her way home.

But it couldn't last; and it was while passing up the coast of Mauritania that Steve became aware of a shortage of free-burning fuel. That in itself wasn't crucial so long as there was sufficient for their needs. However, closer examination of the bunker revealed that coal stocks were drastically depleted, and rather than a wealth of black diamonds what remained was coal-dust and slack. That set the alarm bells ringing and he mentioned the shortfall to the cook.

'Shouldn't worry about it,' said Michael, coolly, as he rolled pastry for a ham and chicken pie. 'If we run out of coal then we'll have to be fed from the main galley.' So, that was Michael's perfunctory attitude; just carry on as usual, hope for the best and if the worst came to the worst so be it - and it wasn't as if they were running out of grub.

And so Steve carried on - until the eve of their arrival at Teneriffe when the world crashed in around his ears. Michael had tended the fire following dinner, banking it up with a shovelful of slack before going for a 'Tennent's' with the 'Chippy'. There was roast pork on the menu for tea; so, having performed his scrub-out Steve placed the joint in the oven then went to his cabin for some shut-eye. All appeared well so what could possibly detract from this unruffled state of affairs. Well, the coal for one thing; for upon his return he found the fire almost out with little hope of it being revived. As was normal, Michael was notable for his absence, although laughter emanating from the Carpenter's cabin indicated that both he and Michael, along with a couple of deckhands, weren't the least bit interested in food.

Steve did the only thing he could, returning to the fire, poking and ruttling, a modern-day, would-be Prometheus. He poked and ruttled, causing any amount of cinders to drop into the ash-pan but with nary a flicker of a flame. He even tried drawing it with a sheet of newspaper but it stubbornly refused to cooperate. The fire was obviously still alight, that much was clear from the tantalising glow at its base; but it just wouldn't burn, owing to it being hopelessly clinkered. Steve took a glance at his watch. It was nearly four o'clock and in just over an hour the peggy would arrive to fetch the tea. Some hopes, thought Steve, who was beginning to panic, knowing that forty hungry men would be more than a handful if their tea wasn't ready when it should be. He'd already peeked into the oven. The joint of supposedly roast pork was much as he'd left it, raw and still cold from the refrigerator. The potatoes were solid, as were the parsnips and sprouts while the Brown Windsor soup, although already made, would still be in need of reheating.

Rather late in the day Steve went in search of his mate because when all was said and done, he was the one who should be cooking the tea and it was he who had banked up the fire. However, when he arrived at the Carpenter's cabin the cabin door was locked although there was the rasp of snoring from within.

'He's sleeping it off,' called a work-stained deckhand, a man whom Steve instantly recognized, and who was applying varnish to a companionway handrail. The bloke was the same miserable creature who'd been manning the gangway when Steve had first joined the *Sombrero*: he was also one of those who earlier in the afternoon had been drinking with Michael and the Chippy.

'Oh, yeah,' replied Steve, indifferently, not giving a toss about the Chippy as Michael was his principal objective. 'And what about the Ships Cook - he sleeping it off too?'

'You can bet your sweet life he is,' answered the seaman, who made way for Steve as the galley boy slipped down the companionway. 'And the way he was staggering back to his cabin you'll not be waking him in a hurry.'

'Come on you piss-head,' cried Steve, shaking Michael for all he was worth, 'the fire's nearly out and it's only another hour till teatime.' But his pleas went completely unheeded, Michael stirring only sufficiently to mutter an off-hand obscenity.

'Fuck off and leave me alone,' he murmured, a contented smile on his face as he rolled over on his side and fell back into a deep drunken sleep.

'Yeah! Okay! I'll leave you alone,' stormed Steve, waving his arms in hopelessness, 'but don't come crying to me when the tea isn't cooked and you end up with a logging.'

Steve stalked out of the cabin, back along the working alleyway, across the after well-deck and up the companionway, brushing past the deckhand and almost kicking over the tin of varnish.

'Hey, look where your fuckin' going,' called the seaman, who'd been shoved against the handrail and now had a broad streak of varnish across the back of his T-shirt, 'it's not my fault he's got himself rotten.'

'Bollocks!' shouted Steve, who suddenly stopped and turned, confronting the man face to face. 'You're as much to blame as he is - you were drinking with him. I bet you didn't tell him it was time he packed it in and thought about cooking your tea.'

The fellow was taken aback and really didn't know what to say. In fact there was little he could say as Steve was essentially correct. Rather than be satisfied with the customary mug of tea for afternoon smoke-ho, the deckhand, along with one of his cronies, had decided on a can of Tennent's of which his pal, the Carpenter, had a caseful. Steve waved a dismissive hand, turning his back on this cretin who was standing open-mouthed and unwittingly varnishing his wristwatch.

An infuriated Steve, meanwhile, still muttering and swearing as he swung through the galley's starboard half-door, almost fell headlong over Whisky who skipped out of the way, staring first at the galley boy and then at his bowl which was empty. 'Oh! Sorry, mate,' apologized Steve, as he knelt down and nuzzled the feline, his cares temporarily dispelled. 'I've been so preoccupied with sorting this other balls-up that I completely forgot about your dinner.'

And so, Whisky got fed, even if - as it seemed - the guys in the mess-room probably wouldn't. In retrospect, Steve should have raked out the fire and remade it - better a late tea than no tea; but he just didn't think and instead began seeking an alternative. It was a fraught situation and he should have sought help but that would have incriminated Michael. Therefore, he rummaged through the fridge in search of a possible solution. And a solution he found - or so he hoped - in the form of tasty Welsh Rarebit that could be easily prepared, courtesy of the electric salamander. Actually, 'Welsh Rarebit' was technically incorrect; but toasted cheese sandwiches were better than nothing even if it wasn't haute-cuisine. There was loads of tinned fruit and plenty of ice-cream so 'pudding' was virtually assured; it just remained for Steve to make the toast.

At five o'clock precisely the peggy appeared with his customary armful of dixies. In normal circumstances he'd make several visits to collect the assortment of fodder; but today wasn't normal as Steve tried gamely to explain. 'You won't be needing that lot tonight,' he advised, apprehensively, as the peggy settled down to listen to what was after all nothing but a load of old bullshit. 'We're running out of coal and the fire's not alight so they'll have to make do with cheese sarnies.......sarnies that have been toasted, mind you.' That much was true, even if the rest of it was crap.

'Ooooh! They're not going to like that,' replied the peggy, ominously, as he loaded the make-shift provender into one of the dixies before departing to relay the sad tidings, 'they enjoy their grub do that lot and this is gonna cause a ruction.'

And that was the inescapable truth - compounded by the fact that the men knew Michael had been drinking. So, it came as no surprise when a few minutes later Graham shouted up from below. 'Hey! Steve!' I thought you ought to know that some of the lads have gone to have a show-down with the cook - and I'll tell you what, they weren't at all happy. I've told the Bosun and he's followed them down to Michael's cabin.'

Sod it, thought Steve, untying the pantry cloth from around his waist and tossing it on to the drainer, I was afraid this was going to happen. 'Okay, Graham,' he called as he slid down the internal companionway and through the sailors' mess-room on his way to find goodness-knows what, 'I'm on my way - although fuck knows what I'm gonna do when I get there.'

To be honest there wasn't much he could do; not with a bunch of angry seamen hell-bent on revenge for their tea being a music-hall joke. In fact he was fearing the worst, even though the Bosun was supposedly on his way to help quell the impending mutiny.

His worst fears were realized when on approaching the cabin he could hear one hell of a rumpus; while the poor old Bosun, whose intentions had been heroic, was slumped in the alleyway nursing a dislocated jaw. Bloody hell, thought Steve, as he arrived at the cabin and surveyed the destruction through the gap where there'd once been a door. There's sod all that I can do here - not without getting a thumping. For destruction there was for the door had been kicked off its hinges leaving the door-jam a mess of torn wood. And amid this devastation stood Michael, his features all battered and bleeding as surrounded by his attackers he wielded a length of split timber. Seeing his mate in such a parlous situation and with further assault seeming imminent, Steve made an on-the-spot decision. He'd seek out the Second Steward; let him sort it out, he reasoned - he's paid a lot more than I am.

'Why do you need me? You're big enough - surely you can deal with something as trivial as an argument.' The Second Steward was standing at the top of the companionway leading to the topside pantry and his response was typical. There was a bloke with a stripe on his sleeve - albeit a solitary zigzag - expecting a low-ranking galley boy to separate two warring factions.

Steve was absolutely livid. 'Not so bloody likely,' he retorted, as the guy with the stripe slipped down from the pantry to discuss the matter directly. 'I'm not getting mixed up in that lot, but if something isn't sorted and sorted pretty quick, I can see the ship's Cook getting slaughtered.'

The Second Steward sighed but he knew what needed to be done. 'Okay, let's go and see what's what - but you know, this ought to teach the bloke a lesson.' And so they fell into step, Steve explaining the circumstances while they headed for the war-zone, not knowing what they'd find when they got there.

But Michael, who by this time had sobered substantially, had given a decent account of himself and had handed out a good deal of punishment. That much was evident by the casualties littering the alleyway; for in addition to the Bosun - who was now on his feet and tentatively caressing his jaw - there was a fireman with a pulverized nose who was crying like a baby because it wouldn't stop bleeding, and a weasel-faced deckie with a bloodied left ear from which sprouted a cruel-looking splinter.

The degree of damage and bloodshed was testament to a huge rough-and-tumble while the threat of further violence still lingered; but for now there was a lull and the Second Steward took full advantage. 'Right, you lot,' he ordered, waving away the majority of the crowd who'd gathered as belligerent onlookers, 'get back to your mess-room and I'll send you some tea from the main galley.' And turning to the injured, he advised, 'You four wait here and I'll send down the Sick-bay Attendant - he'll soon get you all sorted.' Then, rather surprisingly, he took Michael aside and whispered directly in his ear.

'Well! What was that all about?' enquired Steve, the following morning, when Michael rolled up with his face held together with Elastoplast.

'What was what all about?' replied the cook, answering the query with a question.

'Come off it, you know what I'm talking about - that little *'tête-à-tête'* you had with the Second Steward following yesterday's rough-house.'

'Oh! That,' answered Michael, his pummelled features adopting a misshapen grin that must have been absolute agony. 'Only that he wouldn't be reporting the incident - so long as I kept off the booze and didn't cause any further trouble.'

Steve found that quite astonishing; but remarkable though it seemed not a word of the fracas ever found its way to the Captain. It was a classic example of whitewash being used as an art-form. The Sick-bay Attendant was bribed with two-hundred Players; with the caveat that if anything surrounding the incident ever slipped out then his clandestine relationship with one of the 'wingers' would become public. Similarly, the Bosun was placated with a bottle of Bell's while the Chippy was handsomely was rewarded. The latter, although he hadn't been directly involved in the punch-up, received a caseful each of both Tennent's and Tuborg for repairing the shattered cabin door. Every other participant escaped without censure, the entire shemozzle being swept beneath the carpet for the simple reason that everyone - with the exception of the Purser and the Skipper - knew of the Second Steward's lapse in the bond locker.

Not so fortunate was Eileen. Following the call at Teneriffe, where the awnings were again dismantled, she decided to top up her suntan, stripping off on a hatch-cover wearing only the skimpiest of thongs. The trouble was, a middle-aged passenger from Farnham, a fifty-year old spinster who'd never had a man in her life, took offence at the spectacle and reported Eileen to the Purser. The woman, it seemed, had been gazing at Eileen from the lower promenade deck for a good fifteen minutes, admiring the suntanned physique, before suddenly realizing that Eileen wasn't what she thought. The Purser dispatched the Second Steward with orders that Eileen should cover herself up and once respectable, present herself smartly at his office. There followed a severe ticking off with the warning that henceforth, any inappropriate conduct would result in a visit to the Captain.

'Silly old biddy,' complained Eileen, taking a swig from a large gin and orange as she glanced up at the lower promenade deck. 'I ask you - do I look like a piece of fuckin' beefcake? Gawd, she must be frustrated - either that or she's fuckin' short-sighted.'

Steve had received mail at Teneriffe, a letter from his family along with a missive from Maxine. It seemed everyone was anticipating his homecoming; excepting Maxine, of course, who was still dreaming of the day when Steve would come waltzing through the door. And as for Michael: he'd had an aerogramme from Vera who'd been crying her eyes out because Tibbles, her little pet tabby whom she'd had as a kitten, had been flattened by a 101 bus.

'Sounds as if that might solve a problem,' said Michael, as he folded the form and slid it into his left trouser pocket. 'Whisky'll be needing a home - and seeing that Vera loves cats it seems like the ideal solution.'

'What about quarantine?' asked Steve, who didn't like the thought of his little furry friend serving what amounted to a six-month prison sentence. 'Wouldn't he be better off on board?'

'I wouldn't have thought so,' answered Michael, who was now set on the idea of Whisky becoming a proxy for Tibbles. 'There'll be a different bunch of blokes on here next trip and they might not be as kindly as this lot - or he might wander off and become feral. No, I think Vera's the best bet - and as for quarantine, don't even think about it. I'll smuggle him ashore - and if the copper on the gate wants to know what's in the box I'll just bung him a bottle of Jameson's.'

So, that was that, cut and dried; and when Steve gave it thought, Vera seemed the answer to their troubles.

It was said that on a clear day the island of Madeira was visible from seventy miles distant; but by eleven o'clock, and with a planned arrival of around noon, Steve had seen nothing, despite having scoured the northern horizon since daybreak. He was beginning to wonder if the tale about 'being visible from seventy miles away' was a load of old tosh when as if from nowhere, there rose Pico Ruivo, the island's summit, which Steve had mistaken for a cloud-bank. Once again, Mother Nature had fooled him completely. You see, he'd been gazing at the skyline when he should have been staring at the sky. It was another twenty minutes before the shoreline appeared and when it did they were almost on the doorstep.

They arrived off Funchal, the island's capital, as scheduled, the *Sombrero* dropping anchor in the harbour approaches owing to the scarcity of a berth - and there she remained, for the entire duration of her stopover. It was utterly frustrating as the shore was almost within touching distance: red-tiled rooftops amid a kaleidoscope of colour embedded in a verdant oasis. For Madeira was a seaborne terrarium; the 'Floating Garden of the Atlantic' - surrounded by a wilderness of sea. Disappointingly, for the crew at least, the streets were to remain off limits although the passengers were to fare more kindly. They were ferried ashore in a fleet of local boats for a taste of Madeiran hospitality.

Still, the bum-boats offered summary amusement, peddling souvenirs and junk along with a selection of clothing. But none of it was relevant to Steve; the boatmen only dealt in Dollar-bills and Pounds whereas all he could muster was Pesos.

The only cargo to be handled was the aforementioned cork which wasn't what Steve had supposed. Without thinking deeply he'd always considered cork as raw material for 'bottle-stoppers' and of little use for anything else. However, this stuff arrived as rectangular sheets which were loaded directly from scows. 'They use cork for all manner of things,' advised Michael, as they observed the sheets being stowed. 'Flooring, wall-panelling, dartboards, notice-boards, the soles of certain types of shoe - no end of things, including, of course, bottle-stoppers.'

Steve felt a clot as after giving it some thought, weren't the various notice-boards dotted about the *Sombrero* made of this very same substance? Whatever, the loading continued and was completed by late afternoon. The *Sombrero* sailed before the hatches were secured; and by teatime, the only trace of Madeira was the mountain-top high above the clouds.

In normal circumstances the passenger accommodation was forbidden territory for crew unless it was related to their work. However, a visit to the hairdresser was permitted, so long as it was out of hours and they had a prearranged appointment. Steve was in desperate need of a haircut. In fact, it hadn't been cut since that hatchet-job in Woolwich, way back at the beginning of October. The barber, a near eighty-year-old alcoholic who hadn't seen an optician in years had made a right mess of it. And so, on the evening of their departure from Madeira he was given the optimum treatment: haircut, shampoo and scalp-massage, courtesy of Gerald, the *Sombrero's* very own coiffeur. Gerald, being what he was, liked to manipulate his fingers; in a professional capacity, of course, and he knew how to execute a scalp-massage. Thirty-minutes pampering cost two packs of Rothman's which included the purchase of a comb.

Steve, feeling neat and tidy for the first time in weeks, returned to his cabin on a high - to find Jim with his heart in his boots. Alan and Colin were in the rec-room, playing cribbage for ciggies, leaving Jim with the cabin to himself. Alone with his thoughts he'd been reading a letter, an aerogramme with a Buenos Aires postmark that had surprisingly arrived at Madeira. The letter now lay on the table while Jim sprawled across the settee, gazing at the sky through the porthole. 'What are you looking so glum about,' asked Steve, on seeing his pal so unhappy.

Jim glanced up, a wry smile on his lips that did little to hide his dejection. 'Ooooh..........nothing I shouldn't have been prepared for,' he answered, wistfully, picking up the aerogramme and handing it to Steve - a tacit invitation to read it. Steve opened the form and perused its contents, reading it twice in order to grasp its implications, before folding it and handing it back. 'It was no more than I really expected,' continued Jim, as he rose from the settee and blew his nose into a handkerchief, 'but I don't suppose there was any harm in dreaming.'

'No, of course there wasn't,' conceded Steve, who having read the aerogramme now fully understood Jim's depression. 'If you hadn't asked you'd never have known and that would've been even worse.'

'You must have noticed I'd been spending more and more time at the Catholic Mission,' said Jim, as he explained the circumstances surrounding the letter which had been signed by Sister Teresa. 'Well, she said she'd consider it before making up her mind and it seems that's precisely what she did.'

Steve had certainly been aware that Jim had been spending increasing amounts of time in the company of Sister Teresa; but he hadn't known that the fellow had asked the girl to marry him. The air-letter conveyed her decision and it was no wonder that Jim was down-hearted. You see, after careful consideration - talking it over with her Mother Superior along with an area bishop - she'd come to the conclusion that she couldn't marry Jim because she was already married, or would be in the very near future.

Steve didn't truly understand; but apparently, once she'd taken her religious vows she'd not only be married to the Church but more precisely to Christ the Redeemer, such were the ways of the Faith. Jim wasn't sure if she'd taken her vows or if at present it was just an intention; but whatever, it seemed that her mind was made up. 'She tried to explain it to me once,' said Jim, as he sought to enlighten Steve who knew nothing about Catholicism or its sisterhood, 'but it was far and away too complicated. You see, there are so many stages they go through - various vows and so on, at progressive milestones, mostly when they're still pretty young. As I understand it once they've taken their final and most solemn vows then they're committed for life but until then, at least in the earlier days, they can leave the order if they're sure that they can't commit for good.'

'And I don't suppose - what with all these complexities - you know whether she's taken the most solemn vows or not?' asked Steve, trying to get his head around a near impossible conundrum.

'No - I don't,' admitted Jim, who now seemed more perplexed than upset, 'although I'm guessing she hasn't but intends to sooner or later. But it isn't only that. It's this whole thing about devotion to duty - helping others, and so on, because that's the kind of person she is. She'll do anything to help anyone anywhere and as she sees it, being part of a religious order is the best way of achieving her objectives. But - you know, we could have done all of those things together. I told her that I'd leave the sea and find work ashore, even in Buenos Aires, if need be - but it seems as if it just didn't wash. Mind you,' he added, clearly feeling happier for having someone with whom to share his troubles, 'as you read in her letter, if she were to leave the order and get married to anyone then I'd be the one that she'd choose.'

'Well, I suppose that's some consolation,' answered Steve, not knowing for sure if it'd make him any happier if he happened to be standing in Jim's shoes, 'and you never know, there's always a chance she'll change her mind.'

'Huh! Not her,' replied Jim, glancing sideways at Steve as he rummaged around in a drawer. 'You don't know her like I do - once she's made a decision then it's final. Anyway,' he continued, philosophically, having found the clean handkerchief he was looking for, 'it's no use me crying over the inevitable so let's go and have a game of crib.'

Following the call at Lisbon - where shore leave was granted with no adverse repercussions - there began a period of hyper-activity. It commenced that very same evening when a party was held at the behest of the owner, who having purchased his horses in Uruguay was intent on a huge celebration. It was to prove a colossal undertaking as Frederico Henrique surpassed all previous achievements with a banquet befitting of an emperor. It was all hands to the stove and chopping-boards as Steve and Michael, having completed their duties in the crew galley, transferred amidships to assist with the festive preparations. It was midnight before they were finished, utterly fatigued but with six hours overtime to their credit. But not only that; prior to their leaving the galley the owner made a personal appearance, thanking each and every one for their efforts. As a mark of his appreciation he handed Frederico-Henrique a full twenty pounds to be shared between the cooks and their helpers. As was his wont the Chef kept the most - some thirty per-cent - the others receiving diminishing amounts according to experience and rating, with Steve ending up with ten shillings.

The party took place on the Sunday; but there'd be no letting up as the ship was due in London on Thursday. That meant the crew being busy; painting and carrying out additional cleaning that culminated in the fabled 'Channel Night', the final night of the voyage by the end of which all should be polished and sparkling. As previously related, the crew galley had been newly redecorated so painting requirements were minimal; a little 'touching-up', as Michael so succinctly described it. It was the cleaning that required the greater muscle, owing mostly to the coal-dust and smoke which were virtually impossible to prevent. But the final result was spectacular, especially once the stove had been polished - with grate-black and sweat by the bucketful.

'There, the place looks just like a palace,' said Michael, as both he and Steve stood back to admire their handiwork. 'But there's something to remember before we leave the ship otherwise it'll have all been pointless.'

'Oh! And what's that?' asked Steve, absently, waving a pantry cloth to clear a puff of smoke that had leaked from the front of the fire-grill.

'Close the hatch at the foot of the bunker, so that when they load the fuel it doesn't leave the galley like a coal-cellar.'

'You don't have to remind me,' answered Steve, recalling how a couple of months earlier they'd found the galley black owing to his predecessor's negligence. 'I'll make sure that it's shut.'

Michael glanced obliquely at Steve. 'Does that mean you'll be coming back next trip?' he asked, sounding a little surprised, as Steve hadn't mentioned it previously.

'Shouldn't mind,' answered the galley boy, stepping over to the stove to flick away some dust that was threatening to ruin its sparkle, 'but I don't think I'll be coming back as galley boy.'

'Why's that, then?' replied Michael, eyeing up Steve with a squint, as if the answer may have implied something personal. 'My company not good enough for you?'

'Don't be so bloody daft,' countered Steve, knowing that Michael was joking as he playfully nudged him in the ribs. 'No - it's just that it's my eighteenth birthday tomorrow, so from then on they won't be able to employ me as a boy rating.'

'Your eighteen tomorrow?' gasped Michael, who sounded genuinely surprised. 'Why on earth didn't you mention it sooner - we could have had a celebration back in Lisbon.'

That had been the reason for Steve's reticence - so that there shouldn't be any celebration in Lisbon. The last thing they needed was for Michael to get sloshed and end up with another good walloping.

'Still that doesn't stop us celebrating now, does it?' continued the Irishman, piercing two of cans of Tuborg and handing one to Steve before wishing him a premature, 'Happy Birthday'. 'Oh! And before I forget there's another thing. When you fetch the stores can you bring back a large cardboard box?'

For the passengers at least the homeward-bound crossing of the Bay of Biscay was wretched, with the semi-digested remains of Frederico-Henrique's repast - along with those of subsequent intakes - being regularly 'posted' in the toilet. Their misery continued until the *Sombrero* was well into the Channel where the weather relented and their dinners remained in their stomachs. Thankfully, the catering staff weren't affected. They were far too busy to be seasick - not that it was ever very likely - as they went about their chores until late into Channel Night when the additional overtime ceased. As was customary on these occasions the proceedings concluded with 'refreshment' before the men settled down to their packing.

Strangely, and perhaps owing to the fact that the voyage had been of shortish duration, Steve hadn't experienced 'The Channels', that feeling of excitement near the end of a trip when home-thoughts from abroad become uppermost. 'Well, it's not as if we've been on the MANZ run, is it?' observed Michael, referring to the Port Line service that operated between the Canadian eastern seaboard, Australia and New Zealand, and on which the crews were away for many months. 'Or on some battered tramp that only comes home when it has to.' And that was a point worth remembering. When signing on for a deep-sea voyage it was always for a two-year period. In certain instances you might be away for precisely that length of time, or it might be for as little as a month. But whatever; as soon as your ship - whether it be a cargo liner, oil-tanker or tramp - returned to a UK port then the crew were signed off, the voyage being deemed as complete.

They picked up the pilot after dinner, from a Trinity House cutter off Dungeness. The *Sombrero* then continued up Channel; through the Straits of Dover; past the South and North Forelands before arriving in the Thames' lower reaches. While most were asleep she wound her way slowly up the river; past the disfiguring oil-related installations; between the Kent and Essex marshes; past Gravesend and Tilbury until finally, and before daylight had broken, she arrived off the 'Royal' group of docks.

Steve was awoken by the shrill sound of whistles and the cries of loudly-shouted orders. He couldn't just lay there, not with all this going on, so he got up and looked through the porthole. The

Sombrero lay snugly in the lock, tugs fore and aft while men in warm jackets attended to the needs of the moorings. Another thirty minutes and she was in the docks proper with Steve as an avid spectator. It was six twenty-five and he stood by the stove, chatting with Graham who with rain in the air, had slipped into the galley to keep dry. 'Any idea where we're tying up,' he asked, wondering where in the system they'd be berthing.

'Number nine KG5 - so I'm told,' answered the deckhand, as he drew on a Player that glowed like a beacon in the dark, 'between the *Breconshire* and the *City of Karachi*.'

Sod it, thought Steve, that means a bloody long walk to the Connaught bus terminal. He'd no intention of paying a quid into the kitty for a ride in one of the limousines that ferried home-going crew to the various mainline railway stations. He was taking care of his money; and he could get to King's Cross by bus and underground for more or less the price of a pint.

The heaving lines were already laid out, waiting to be thrown, and the lads stood nattering until the order was given that the deckies should take up their docking stations. 'Anyway, gotta go,' said the lanky Australian as he hurried outside to play his part in the voyage's completion', 'I'll have a quick word with you later.'

By this time Michael had arrived, and was busy punching holes in the large cardboard box that Steve had acquired from the dry stores. 'There, that should do him,' said the cook, staring fondly at Whisky who lay snoozing in front of the fire. 'And whatever you do, don't let him out in case he decides to do a runner.'

From that point on it was bedlam. Cook the breakfast; gobble their own meals; rake out the fire and safely dispose of the ashes before cleaning the galley - and all this before the really serious business of signing off and collecting their wages. But on a more positive note; once they were finished they wouldn't have to wait for relief.

Whisky was a discontented puss. On several occasions he tried to escape but each time he was comfortably foiled. His best opportunity was when Steve went to empty the rosie; but despite the fact that he was as slippery as an eel, Michael held firm and he was safely ensconced in his box. There was loads of miaowing and scratching but to no avail; he was heading for Vera's and there was nothing in the world he could do about it. Of course, Steve had given him a cuddle and plenty of fussing, knowing that would be the last he'd see of him. In fact, he'd even shed a tear; but he was cheered by the knowledge that the cat would be lovingly cared for. Whisky eventually settled, accepting his fate which in the final analysis - and as Graham rightly said - would be regarded by Australians as - 'Bonza'.

'Well, I'm going to get washed and changed,' said Michael, picking up the box which was bound with a strong length of twine. And glancing at the foot of the coal bunker he added, 'And don't forget to close that hatch.

Ahhh! - yes, thought Steve, as he crossed to the bunker and slid down the hatch-cover until it wouldn't slide any further. Talk about sailing on a knife edge. They'd got home by the skin of their teeth. There'd been just enough coal to cook the porridge and eggs with a shovelful of slack as insurance. But that was all now potted history. There'd be no dinner or tea to worry about; all that remained was to empty the fridge before finally securing the galley.

'Do you fancy coming back next trip?' asked Frederico Henrique, when Steve handed over the keys. 'There'll be a vacancy for a Cook's Assistant if you're interested. Michael happened to mention that you were eighteen on Tuesday so you'll have effectively gained your rating.'

Was Steve interested? You could bet your life he was - but what about Colin and Alan?

'You don't have to worry about them,' advised the Chef, now confident his offer would be accepted. 'Colin said he fancied a change - a trip to the 'States' if he could get one, and Alan's still only seventeen.'

'Thanks, Fred,' replied Steve, using the shortened form of the man's Christian name for the first time ever, rather than the more formal, 'Chef', 'I'd love to come back - I couldn't wish for anything better.'

With the exception of Colin and the Assistant Baker - who'd been offered a shore job with 'Hovis' - it seemed the main galley crew would be staying. That meant Steve would be working with Jim who despite the refusal from Sister Teresa seemed determined to carry on trying. All in all it seemed there were exciting times ahead - and his pay will have been greatly enhanced.

So, that was his future taken care of but what should he do in the meantime? Well, get showered and changed for one thing and then say 'cheerio' to his mates. The *Sombrero* would be signing off in the officers' and engineers' dining room from eleven o'clock onwards so he really ought to get his skates on.

'See you in a couple of weeks, then,' said Steve, addressing the reliable Graham, who obviously wasn't going home but would be one of the few working by. 'And thanks for looking after Whisky.'

'Don't mention it - it was a pleasure,' answered the deckhand, who despite the fact that the ship was paying off was touching up some paintwork in the mess-room. 'And I'm sure he'll be fine - even if Vera is a dipso.'

'I'm certain you're right,' answered Steve, raising a hand as he stepped over the coaming and out on to the after well-deck, 'and with Michael back aboard we're sure to get regular updates.'

Twenty-Six Pounds, four-shillings and eleven-pence, all for a couple of month's work. Actually, when he totalled it all up; basic rate, overtime and leave pay, he'd grossed nearly twice that amount but stoppages had greatly reduced it. That said, four pounds a month had been paid to his bank in the form of an allotment; periodical savings and a foundation for his fare to New Zealand. He'd drawn an advance on his pay and subbed in BA not to mention his on-board purchases; essentials mainly, such as cigarettes, toothpaste and detergent. He'd settled some arrears with the union rep but that apart, the money that was left was his own. Okay, he'd have to give a fiver to his Mum, for board and lodgings, and so on, but all things considered it was a decent return for his first ever voyage in the *Sombrero*.

'How are you going to get him back to Cyprus with all that luggage?' demanded Steve, staring at the cardboard box that was surrounded by cases and holdalls. Michael and Derek were swigging from cans of Tennant's, farewell 'bevvies' to tide them over till the next time.

'No worries, Sonny Boy,' answered the cook, cheerfully, raising his can as a salute to his erstwhile workmate. 'I'll be taking a taxi - surely you don't think I'd be daft enough to try and carry this lot.'

Derek - who at the outset had been far from enamoured with the Irishman but was now one of his favourite drinking companions - also hoisted his can, slopping some of its contents over Michael. 'You don't have to worry about him,' he slavered, suppressing a fit of the giggles. 'He's as steady and as sensible as they come...........sometimes.'

Steve rolled his eyes, easing the door shut behind him. It seemed everything aboard was as normal.

EPILOGUE

In the early 1960s some thirty-odd per-cent (not sixty per-cent as erroneously quoted in the preface to 'Sunshine, Sugi and Salt') of the world's merchant tonnage flew the flag of the British Merchant Navy. At the time it was the largest merchant navy in the world and the flag was the Red Ensign - known affectionately as, 'The Red Duster'. Vessels flying the Red Duster could be found almost everywhere with a host of British shipping companies - some of them single-ship affairs while others comprised numerous vessels - serving all five continents. Indeed, the post-war years, through the 'fifties' and 'sixties', were considered by many to have been the British shipping industry's golden era. They were halcyon days for the British seafarer whose lot had never been better; and looking back on their time at sea most would view those years fondly. Despite the inevitable grumblings - which were largely unjustified and came mostly from bellyachers and agitators - pay and conditions compared favourably with most jobs ashore and with few exceptions included a man's board and lodging. There were even those, especially among the younger generation - although they wouldn't have admitted it at the time - who considered themselves wage-earning tourists, travelling at the shipowners' expense. In truth, the British merchant seafarer of the post-war period was frequently the envy of many, who for whatever reason - perhaps family commitments or a certain faint-heartedness - chose to remain on terra firma.

So, given this rosy situation what on earth could have gone so horribly wrong that within a brief twenty years the majority of that fleet had disappeared, and with it the seamen who'd sailed it?

I won't be indulging in politics, other than to suggest that given Britain's eminent position in terms of international commerce then maybe a cocktail of complacency; the age-old British reluctance to invest in anything 'untested' - preferring instead to stick with tradition while saving money into the bargain - along with perhaps the seamen's strike of 1966 which did little to help at a time when stability was of the essence, were all contributory factors. Whatever, Britain clearly missed out on the boom in containerization and ro-ro, preferring instead to adhere with what she knew best. So, while American, Asian and European operators poured money into sleek modern tonnage the British persisted with convention - if they invested at all.

From the late-sixties onwards attempts were made to arrest this decline in fortunes. There were amalgamations that saw the disappearance of some of the most familiar names in the industry. This was accompanied by a belated entry into the container market with Cunard, P&O and Blue Star arguably in the forefront. Others simply fell by the wayside, going out of business altogether while other famous names were swallowed up; mostly by overseas operators, often resulting in extinction.

But whatever the whys and wherefores, disappear they did so that today only about three per-cent of the world's tonnage actually flies the Red Ensign with most of the owners being anonymous. Foreign seamen - largely from the Philippines, Indonesia and Eastern Europe - form the crews; and good luck to them, I say. And that, dare I suggest, was the catalyst; cheap foreign labour along with sub-standard working and living conditions that no British seaman would tolerate - and nor should he have been expected to. So there you have it as the author sees it. You may agree or disagree; but whatever the reasons a unique way of life has disappeared, almost certainly never to return.

Inevitably, the collapse of the British shipping industry had a profound effect on the ports and communities it had supported. Taking London - in the 'fifties' and 'sixties' the largest seaport in the world - as an example: entire areas of the East End, from the Pool of London in the west to North Woolwich in the east - including the 'Surrey' side of the river - saw livelihoods disappear as docks were closed and more modern facilities commissioned, either further down stream or around the estuary, to cater for the new foreign-owned operators.

Shops, public houses and a host of other small enterprises went out of business as the trade they relied on evaporated. Nowhere was this more apparent than in the pubs, that had rang to the chatter and laughter of generations of seamen and dockworkers since London first evolved as a port, only to fall silent with only a few 'locals' remaining. Gone were the likes of The Roundhouse, The Central, The Royal Oak, The Gallion's Hotel and goodness knows how many more, now either shuttered and closed, converted for other purposes and in some cases demolished altogether.

Some of these neighbourhoods have since flourished. We've all heard of Canary Wharf, the site of the erstwhile West India and Millwall Docks, now redeveloped; a high-rise centre of finance, commerce and home to city workers, mostly those on high salaries. The Surrey group of docks - now largely filled in - along with the upper docks and riverside warehouses, have all succumbed to the developer, transformed into either waterside apartments or for leisure purposes. North Woolwich and the area surrounding the Royal Docks, by comparison, might rightly be described as a wasteland. There are those who'd obviously disagree; the planners, politicians and developers, for instance, who'd point to the London City Airport, the Docklands Light railway and the ExCeL Centre at Custom House as examples of regeneration. But once again, it's the well-heeled who've reaped the rewards, leaving unswept streets and derelict infrastructure in the areas that have been so far neglected. There's little doubt, in the author's mind at least, that in the fullness of time North Woolwich will itself see changes. Whether or not the locals will benefit is a different matter; although being downstream from the Thames Barrier, with the associated climate-change issues, one has to wonder if the 'money' will be so readily tempted.

As for places overseas: like most capital cities Buenos Aires has seen many changes. Steve Chapman, for instance, wouldn't recognise the area around La Boca which with its brightly-coloured, sheet-metal buildings has been transformed into a tourist attraction. Efforts have even been made to clean up the Rio Riachuelo and the La Vuelta de Rocha lagoon, with waterside walks and pavement cafés designed to attract moneyed visitors. The Puenta Nicolás Avellaneda still stands, as does the Puenta Transbordador, although they are now accompanied by a motorway flyover linking Buenos Aires with the city of La Plata. As for the Refrigorifico Anglo: the abattoir and meat-packing plant was closed and demolished in the 1970s and it is probably safe to assume that the 'Nash' and the Welcome Bar went with it. The site is now occupied by an up-to-date container-handling facility.

So, what of Steve Chapman and the *Sombrero*. Well, Steve did return to the *Sombrero,* completing half-a-dozen trips in total; the first two as Cooks' Assistant before further promotion saw him engaged as Assistant Cook. And then came the unexpected death sentence. Upon her return from Buenos Aires in January 1964 her owners decreed that the *Sombrero* was to be de-commissioned. In common with passenger ships everywhere the jet airliner was beginning to eat into her profit margins; and so, given her advanced age the Simpson Line had decided to dispose of her. There were those who couldn't have cared less, considering the scrapyard as appropriate, while others were aghast at the announcement, wondering how they were going to survive. Indeed, for some of the crew, certain members of the catering staff for instance and the likes of Georgina in particular, she was the only home that they knew. They might be all right in the short term, finding work aboard other vessels, but it was gradually dawning that this was the beginning of the end and that other forms of lifestyle beckoned.

Steve fell somewhere in between. He would be sorry to witness her passing; but in the months since gaining his rating he'd saved sufficient to pay his way to New Zealand. He therefore took the plunge, firstly initiating the migration process with the authorities at the New Zealand High Commission. He then wrote to Maxine - who was elated at the news - informing her that he was on his way and that if all went to plan he should be in Manoao by July. On receiving the 'all clear' from New Zealand House, all that remained was to book his passage on the earliest available sailing.

The *Sombrero,* meanwhile, was stripped of everything recyclable; crockery and cutlery, etc. - and anything that could be used aboard other Simpson Line vessels - before sailing from London for the final time as the last snows of winter were melting. She first went to Falmouth in Cornwall where items such as beds, armchairs, tables and sofas; indeed, anything that could be sold and was of no further use, was removed and auctioned on the quayside. And then she was away to Barcelona where the acetylene torches were waiting. It was an ignominious end for a faithful old ship and many regretted her passing, not least Steve who shed more than a tear as he took his last steps down her gangway.

And Steve? He arrived in Manoao in the June. The welcome was out of this world with Maxine's parents, Frank and Margaret fêt-ing him as a long-lost son. The romance was immediately rekindled - not that it needed rekindling - and he and Maxine were married in the week before Christmas. He initially worked in the store, alongside Maxine and Margaret. However, what with Frank being a nifty motor mechanic with ambitions of branching out into the taxi business, it wasn't long before Steve was behind the wheel of a cab. As the years rolled by Steve and Maxine - who by this time had two growing children - gradually took over the workload while Margaret and Frank 'took it easy', Frank with his fishing and Margaret with her hobby of embroidery. The passing decades were kind; notwithstanding the inevitable hiccups that life throws up along the way. So, now in his seventieth year and himself retired Steve could look back on a life of memorable accomplishment. He had a fantastic wife and a family that was the envy of many. The business had prospered under his and Maxine's stewardship so whom should he thank for these 'riches'? After some serious reflection it soon became abundantly clear. The *Vindicatrix* had certainly played her part; in character building, and so on, helping him cope in tight corners or when winds weren't blowing in his favour. However, he knew in his heart that he owed the greatest debt of all to his parents, for allowing him to go to sea in the first place.

Incidentally, while it was still commonplace for some British freighters of the 'fifties' and 'sixties' to be equipped with a coal-fired galley it wasn't usually the case aboard passenger ships, even when catering for the crew. However, the fact that some examples did exist meant that the *Sombrero* wasn't unique. Indeed, the crew areas aboard all four of Blue Star's premier post-war passenger-carrying vessels: *Argentina Star, Brasil Star, Paraguay Star* and *Uruguay Star,* were similarly provided. Those vessels that were equipped with coal-fired cooking facilities could usually be identified by the 'H-shaped' chimney protruding from the relevant area of the superstructure.

Over the years the River Plate estuary has witnessed more than its share of disasters, with none more tragic than that alluded to in chapter eight of this volume.

At around 5.30am on the foggy morning of 11th May 1972 the Houlder Bro's cargo liner *Royston Grange,* loaded with chilled beef and dairy produce, collided with the Liberian-registered tanker *Tien Chee* in the Punta Indio Channel. The *Royston Grange* was only a few hours into her homeward-bound voyage while the oil-laden tanker was in bound. As a result of the collision, escaping oil from the *Tien Chee* became quickly alight, igniting a cloud of vapour that had enveloped the Houlder Line vessel. The ensuing fireball killed her entire complement; 61 crew, 12 passengers (including a child), along with her Argentine pilot. Eight of the tanker's crew of 40 also perished. It is thought the fire was so intense that those aboard the British ship, most of whom were asleep, died without knowing of their fate.

R.I.P.

GLOSSARY OF SHIPBOARD TERMS, some of which appear in this volume.

AB: *Able Seaman.*

Accommodation Ladder: *Gangway from ship to shore.*

Aft: *Rear section of ship (Tourist section on many passenger liners).*

Articles: *Terms of agreement between shipmaster and crew.*

AS: *Assistant Steward usually referred to as,' Steward'.*

Athwartships: *From port to starboard and reverse.*

BA: *Buenos Aires.*

Bibby Alleyway: *Cul – de-Sac.*

Bloods: *Passengers.*

Blues: *Navy Blue Uniform.*

BOT: *Board of Trade.*

Boss: *Chief Steward (Also Purser).*

BR: *Bedroom Steward.*

Bulkheads: *Walls.*

Commis: *Apprentice Waiter (Passenger Liners).*

Companionway: *Staircase.*

Cover: *A complete set of table cutlery.*

Deadlight: *Metal cover over porthole.*

Deck: *Floor.*

Deckhead: *Ceiling.*

Dhobi: *Washing clothes.*

Ducer: *Second Steward.*

Duty Mess: *set-aside dining area where duty engineers could eat out of uniform.*

EDH: *Efficient Deckhand.*

For'ard: *Forward section of ship.*

Fiddle: *Raised edge around table top to prevent items sliding off in rough weather.*

Heads: *Crew toilets.*

JOS: *Junior Ordinary Seaman.*

KG5: *King George V Dock.*

Leading Hand: *Petty Officer.*

Lecce: *Electrician.*

Lockerman: *Steward in charge of lockers; e.g. Cruet locker, Silver locker, fruit locker, etc. (Passenger liners).*

Maindeckman: *Steward in charge of Second Steward's gear (Passenger liners).*

MOT: *Ministry of Transport.*

Overheads: *Ledges, pipes, beams, etc., above the head.*

Peak (Also 'Glory Hole'): *Steward's accommodation (Passenger Liners).*

Pig & Whistle: *Crew bar (Passenger liners).*

PLA: *Port of London Authority.*

Port side: *Left side of ship facing forward.*

Returns: *Repeat food orders/ Second helping of dish.*

Rosie: *Refuse bin.*

Rounds: *Captain's inspection (Chief Officer if Master unavailable).*

Running sitting: *Continuous service of meal (Passenger liners).*

Scupper: *Drain.*

Scuttle: *Porthole.*

Seven-bell breakfast: *Seven-thirty am breakfast for officers and engineers on eight till twelve watch.*

Sheds: *Passenger's cabins or staterooms.*

Show: *Waiter's table section (Passenger liners).*

Side doors: *Doors in side of ship used for when passengers are embarking or disembarking. Also used for taking aboard stores (Usually passenger liners).*

Side job: *Working routine between meals (Catering staff).*

Silver: *Table cutlery, etc.*

Slops: *Clothing, shoes and other items available for sale to crew.*

Smoke-ho: *Morning and afternoon breaks for deck and engine room crew.*

SOS: *Senior Ordinary Seaman.*

Sparky: *Radio Officer (Not electrician).*

Sub: *Allowance from pay.*

Sugi (Sometimes 'Soogee'): *Hot soapy water.*

Strapping up: *Washing dishes, silver, pots and pans, etc.*

Single change: *Changing one sheet or pillow case only on a bed or bunk.*

Starboard: *Right side of ship facing forward.*

Swing the lamp: *Reminisce.*

Tabnabs: *Cakes and pastries.*

Topside: *Upper decks on a ship (First class on passenger liners).*

Tiger: *Captain's personal steward.*

Tick on: *Report for duty (Mostly, but not always, aboard passenger liners)*

Tramp or Tramp Steamer: *A freighter with no regular route or itinerary. She literally 'tramps' the oceans in search of any profitable cargo.*

Well-deck: *Open space on the main deck of a ship where cargo hatches are located, usually fore and aft of the central accommodation area.*

Whites: *White tropical uniform.*

Winger: *Waiter (Mostly passenger liners).*

Working alleyway: *Alleyway off which a vessel's principal working areas are located: galley, storerooms, etc. Also, mostly aboard cargo vessels, off which catering staff accommodation is situated.*

Printed in Great Britain
by Amazon